THE NIGHT WE MET A DRAGON

by A. R. Marshall

www.armarshall.com/storykeeping

STORY KEEPING SERIES

BOOK TWO

To my wife, Janay

"Perfect love drives out all fear."

I love your love.

*Note to Parents – FREE Audiobook!

Thanks! You're going to love the Story Keeping Series!

As a token of my thanks I'm offering the AUDIOBOOK, *The Night I Became A Hero*, for FREE to my readers. I'll also keep you up to date on upcoming releases, special deals, and other freebies...

*earbuds not included

Download for free at

www.armarshall.com/storykeeping

Here's what readers are saying about the Story Keeping Book Series!

"It's fun, full of adventure, and I can't wait to read the next book!"

Samara, 9

"The story immediately pulled me in on a magnetic, compelling journey and didn't let go – dynamically weaving in surprises and subtleties. It's an absolute winner for any age."

Mike, 38

"So good it makes me speechless!"

Maddie, 7

"My kids immediately asked me to start reading the next book in the series when we finished Story Keeping, Book 1."

Rick, 36

"I loved the adventure, I hope you write a billion more books like this!"

Aricin, 8

Table of Contents

Preface

Hi. My name is Riles.

Did you miss my first story – about the time we saved Space Spy Drift Elwick from intergalactic space pirates?

Let me catch you up.

I am a *hero*. Seriously.

Not a *superhero*.

I can't fly. I don't have super speed, x-ray vision, plastic arms, or super strength either.

In fact, I'm a pretty normal fifth grader in almost every way except one – I'm a *Story Keeper*.

Have you ever heard of *Story Keeping*? That's okay, neither had I – until that first summer at grandpa's house.

Ever since I can remember, Sissie, Finn and I have spent one week each summer at grandpa's house. Mom and dad drop us off at the beginning of the week and pick us up seven days later.

Over the years, we've enjoyed amazing adventures with grandpa – treasure hunts, night hikes, star-gazing, and s'mores around the backyard fire pit.

This summer was different. Grandpa took our adventures to a whole new level. (You can read about how it all started in my first story – *The Night I Became A Hero*.)

He introduced us to *Story Keeping*.

So, what is *Story Keeping*?

Well, you know how most stories have happy endings? They don't always start that way – happy endings aren't guaranteed.

There are even people out there trying to ruin stories – trying to steal the happy ending. Crazy, right?

Those stories need help. That's where *Story Keeping* comes in – we protect stories and save happy endings.

I know, it sounds kind of nutty, but it's true. Grandpa says people in our family have been saving stories for centuries. He learned *Story Keeping* from his mom, and she learned it from one of her great uncles.

Now, Sissie, Finn and I are learning.

For example, in Drift's story we learned three important story keeping lessons:

1. We can send messages to characters in the story. A few times when we shouted at the book, it flashed bright white.

Then, someone in the book found a note that said whatever we had shouted.

2. We learned that sometimes the book can suck you in – literally. I was reading and when my finger touched the page I got pulled right into the story. Next thing I knew, I was face-to-face with Space Spy Drift Elwick, in a vent, inside a giant spaceship, somewhere between Mars and Jupiter.

3. We learned that sometimes you can move around inside a book by *wishing* yourself to a new place. We learned that trick from Lark.

Okay, are you all caught up? Great! Let's jump into the next adventure.

1

Dragon Cover

"Hurry up – It's 7:58!" Sissie hollered from her middle bunk.

"We're going as fast as we can!" I shouted back, spraying toothpaste foam all over the sink and bathroom mirror.

I glanced at Finn, who brushed his teeth frantically, next to me. Drool covered his face. We only had two more minutes. No way was I missing story time tonight:

Shower – check,

Pajamas on – check,

Room picked up – check,

Teeth brushed – working on it!

It had been three nights since our first "story keeping" adventure with grandpa and we were beyond excited for another chance – for another magical book! For the last two days, all Sissie, Finn, and I had talked about was the adventure with Drift.

Grandpa kept hinting that he had more books that needed "keeping." The three of us could hardly contain our excitement!

We wanted to start another book the very next night, but grandpa had friends over for dessert. They left after bedtime, so we didn't get a chance to read. Last night we stayed up too late playing games.

Tonight, grandpa said we had to be ready for bed by eight o'clock or we wouldn't have enough time to read the bedtime story.

We had to be ready by eight.

I grabbed a small towel to wipe toothpaste foam off of my face – and Finn's. Then, the two of us rushed into our bunks as Sissie yelled for grandpa:

"We're ready!"

Grandpa didn't yell back, but we could hear his footsteps coming down the hall. My heart pounded inside my chest – all that racing around to finish chores. We made it.

Pausing at the door, grandpa smiled. A few nights ago, while reading about Space Spy Drift Elwick, grandpa did a lot of winking and smiling. I think he liked story time almost as much as us kids. Especially these books.

Now, he stood in the doorway holding his cup of tea – and a new book.

Sissie and Finn noticed the book too:

"Whoa, grandpa!" Finn blurted out in a loud whisper, "Cool book."

The dark-green cover looked dusty and old, like Drift's story. Grandpa walked toward our triple bunk bed holding the book at his side.

"Children," he spoke softly, "This book has been in our family for many generations. It's been one of *my* favorite adventures for years – since I attended grade school. In fact, my grandmother first read it with me when I was about your age, Riles."

"Really?" I asked in a whisper.

Grandpa nodded.

"Have mom and dad ever read this book?" whispered Finn, looking at the dragon on the cover.

"They have," grandpa replied in a distant voice, "They most certainly have."

"Can we?" Sissie followed.

"Yes, of course, sweetheart," grandpa replied with a chuckle, "That's why I brought it up tonight."

"What's it about grandpa?" Finn asked from the bottom bunk.

Grandpa smiled, "I don't want to spoil the fun, but, I can tell you this: it's got everything a good story needs – a villain, a hero, and a few surprises. Would you like to take a closer look?"

"Yes," all three of us blurted out, excited for another incredible adventure.

Grandpa held out the book so that each of us could see the cover. It was beautiful. A strange creature filled the cover – zig-zagging its scaly body across the leather binding. It had detailed scales and two large wings. The book looked old. Up close you could hear it humming – like it was alive. I couldn't tell for sure in the dim light of the room, but the creature on the cover seemed to move — ever so slightly — as grandpa held out the book.

Tucking the book back under his arm, grandpa headed to his rocking chair. He placed the steaming cup of tea on his side table, sat down in his rocker, and positioned the dark-green book in his lap.

"Shall we begin?" grandpa asked.

"Absolutely!" we all answered.

All three of us were bursting with excitement. After two full days of waiting, the next adventure was finally here!

Grandpa balanced the book in the middle of his lap — on its binding. Maybe my eyes were playing tricks on me, but the creature on the cover definitely looked like it was moving — slithering back and forth around the leather cover. Even though the book was still closed, its pages began to glow with a soft white light.

As grandpa pulled his hands away, the book fell open in his lap. The pages shuffled themselves left and right – all by itself – and the soft glow grew. We watched, wide-eyed with surprise. Grandpa paid little attention to the magical book. He took a sip of tea as it shuffled back and forth. Then, he set his mug back, pulled reading glasses from his shirt pocket, unfolded them, and placed them on his nose. The book's soft white light reflected off his glasses.

Grandpa's eyes scanned the shuffling pages.

"Alright, where do you want us to start reading this time?"

"How about the beginning?" I laughed.

"I wasn't asking you, Riles, I was asking the book," Grandpa smiled.

The pages slowed, then another page turn, then the soft glow pulsed.

We all sat on the edge of our bunks – speechless at the wonder of this magical book.

"Isn't that interesting," grandpa muttered.

Then, he began to read.

2

The Prince

"Let me out of here!" Winthrop shouted again.

There was no reply.

Exhausted from yelling, Winthrop let go of the iron bars and slumped onto to the dirt floor – tired, cold, and lonely. He tugged at a thick leather bracelet wrapped tight on his left wrist, and glanced at the rock wall to his right – eight chalk lines etched in the stone wall.

Scratching at his wrist, he counted the chalk marks again. For eight long nights, he had been trapped in this dark hole. How long would he have to wait?

His eyes were already used to the darkness. Aside from a few oil lamps flickering along the deeper paths, no light snuck into this cave.

The boy counted days in the dark by meals. Two times each day a guard, bearing the symbol of the Kingdom – a mighty oak tree on his armor and helmet – carried a single tray of food to Winthrop. Every time the guard would arrive and leave without saying a word.

Far away, the scaly beast never seemed to sleep.

"Let me go!" Winthrop shouted again, this time from the cold floor of his prison cell.

Looking away from the iron bars, Winthrop glanced at the flat wooden tray.

"This is supposed to be lunch?" He muttered to himself.

A boiled onion, a bread roll, and water – again. Winthrop grunted in disgust.

"You'll pay for this!" he yelled into the darkness.

"Silence!" A deep roar echoed loudly. Even the oil lamps rattled with fear at the rush of warm air.

***

"Was that a dragon?" Finn interrupted.

"I'm not sure, would you like to find out?" grandpa replied.

"Wait a minute, you *do* know, don't you?" I caught grandpa's attention. "Didn't you say that you've read this book before."

Grandpa chuckled and looked up from the book.

"I suppose I do know the answer, don't I," he replied.

Looking toward Little Finn, grandpa added "You don't want me to ruin the story for you, do you?"

"No, I guess not," Finn said with a smile.

Looking back at me, grandpa continued, "Keep in mind, Riles, that these are not ordinary stories. As you learned a few nights ago in Drift's story, these stories can take on a life of their own. Sometimes they take twists and turns that I don't even expect."

The book's white glow pulsed brighter.

"It seems like the book is eager for us to read more. Shall we continue the story?" Grandpa asked, looking over his glasses at each of us.

We all nodded in agreement.

Grandpa continued.

***

Winthrop shuddered at the sound of that horrible voice. He picked up the boiled onion and tried to take a bite. Awful.

He tried the bread. Hard as a rock.

If only he wasn't so hungry.

18

Winthrop choked down the rest of another terrible meal. Then, he got back to planning his escape. He had been waiting – for a sign, or a note. He simply had to get out, and fast.

Looking away from the chalk marks, Winthrop glanced toward the pile of stones he had collected in the corner. He scratched at his wrist and imagined his escape. His plan just might work, but he really needed the old beast to fall asleep.

Far from Winthrop – deep in the mountain, laying on mounds of gold and jewels – an ancient, scaly, green dragon stretched his dark wings in the dim light of his cave.

"Pesky pest of a boy," Vilgor muttered to himself in disgust, "I'll be glad when this is over."

Then, the scaly beast curled up like a puppy, tucked his wings close to his side, shut his large golden eyes, and began to dream.

Beyond Winthrop's cell and far from Vilgor's plunder – outside the dark cave and deep in the forest, at the mountain's feet – a handful of men sat around a small fire.

Flickering flames lit their dirty, bearded faces and beady eyes. Dressed in dark cloaks, hiding daggers and bows, the men grumbled and complained at each other. They seemed angry and frustrated.

"We cannot go into the mountain."

"But he must be freed, and we must free him!"

"Without him, our plan will fail."

"Are you suggesting we face the dragon?"

"Face the dragon? No."

"Are you a coward?"

"Careful who you call a coward, boy."

"How then? Vilgor will destroy us if we try to enter his mountain."

"There must be another way."

"We cannot fight the dragon!"

Finally, a man named Devlin stood and interrupted their arguing. He shouted:

"Silence. Stop your complaining."

***

Suddenly, Grandpa paused.

"Devlin?" he muttered under his breath, "What is he doing in this..."

"What's that grandpa?" I interrupted.

"Huh?" grandpa looked up – like he had barely heard me, "Oh, nothing Riles. Where was I?"

And, grandpa continued reading.

***

The arguing stopped as the men turned toward Devlin.

One of them, a strong woodsman named Brison, replied:

"Stranger, take a seat. You are in our forest, talking about our mountain, and our dragon."

"Yes, of course," Devlin replied, "But remember, I have invited you to this fire – not the other way around."

"Hmmph," Brison grumbled back, "Speak quickly, then, I am already losing patience."

"Very well," Devlin continued, "Listen carefully. I will explain my plan. But first, let us remember why we are here – to free the Prince from that vile beast."

3

Grandpa Knows

"Wait," Sissie jumped in, "Did he say free the Prince?

"He did," grandpa replied.

"From the vile beast," I added.

"Yep," grandpa nodded.

"Okay," Sissie said, "I have a question."

"Go on." grandpa asked.

"Vilgor is the dragon, right?"

"Yeesss," Finn hollered impatiently from the bottom bunk, "Can we get back to the story?"

"Aaannnnddd," Sissie went on, "These guys want to help a prince break get away from a vile beast, right?"

"Hold on," I jumped in, "Is Winthrop the prince?"

Grandpa smiled.

"He must be," Sissie answered, which means Vilgor is the vile beast!"

This book sounded a lot like your classic medieval fairy tale. If the evil dragon was holding the prince prisoner, we could *totally* help him.

"I get it!" Finn added, "So our job is to help Winthrop get away from Vilgor!"

Grandpa tilted his head.

"I think so!" Sissie replied, "Winthrop already has a plan – he's just waiting..."

"For the dragon to fall asleep!" Sissie, Finn, and I all shouted together.

"Hold on kids," grandpa tried to slow us down, "Are you sure you want…"

"Hey Winthrop," Finn interrupted, *"The dragon is asleep!"*

"…to do that?" grandpa's voice trailed off.

Bright white light pulsed from the book.

Sissie and I both leaned out of our bunks. We looked at Finn, then grandpa, then Finn.

"What?" Finn asked sheepishly, "We wanted to help the prince, right?"

"Um, I think so," I replied. "What do you think, grandpa?"

Grandpa sighed.

"I'm not sure, kids. You certainly did a good job of putting the clues together. It sounds like Vilgor *is* the dragon, and it sounds like he *has* locked up Prince Winthrop."

"And, we helped him, right?" Finn added.

"Based on the white flash of light," grandpa replied, "I think we probably sent a clue to Winthrop – a clue that will probably help him escape."

"That's good, right grandpa?" Sissie asked.

"Probably."

"Probably?" Little Finn asked.

"What do you mean probably, grandpa?" I asked. "I thought we were supposed to help save the story – isn't that what story keeping is all about?"

Grandpa paused for a moment. He chose his words carefully.

"You're right, Riles. Our job *is* to help save stories," grandpa said. "Sometimes, though, it's difficult to know who in the story we ought to be helping."

"What do you mean, grandpa?" Sissie asked.

Then it hit me.

"Like Lark?" I asked.

"Yes, like Lark," grandpa replied.

Lark was this girl in our first adventure who – spoiler alert – didn't really want to help Space Spy Drift Elwick save Earth. She fooled us all.

"Oh, Lark made me so mad!" Little Finn piped in from the bottom bunk. "She pretended to be Drift's friend and turned out to be awful!"

"Yes, Finn," grandpa added, "People aren't always as they seem."

"What about dragons?" Sissie asked.

"Yeah," Finn added. "Dragons are always bad, right?"

"Perhaps even dragons should be given a chance," grandpa replied.

"Really?" I asked.

"Perhaps."

Probably? Perhaps? Grandpa definitely knew more about this story than he was telling us. It made me wonder what secrets he was keeping – and why.

"Should we get back to reading?" Grandpa asked.

We all nodded.

Looking back at the book, he muttered, "Where are we? Ah yes, here we go."

***

"I know a man," Devlin replied, "who knows a secret way into the mountain."

"Impossible," the men grumbled to each other, "There is only one road leading into the mountain."

Then, at the edge of the wood, the men heard leaves rustling. Jumping to their feet, weapons drawn, they listened.

More leaves rustled at the edge of the forest, and then a slippery voice spoke out of the darkness:

"I am that man. I know another way into the mountain."

His voice made the hair on their necks stand up straight.

"Who goes there? Show yourself," the men shouted.

"Easy gentlemen, I have invited him," Devlin replied.

"Yes. You heard him," the slippery voice spoke again. "I am an invited guest."

A hooded figure walked slowly from the edge of the forest toward the flickering firelight. He stopped at the edge of their circle and took a seat on a tree stump. The men stepped back.

Crackling flames threw dim red light onto his hooded face. He looked wrinkled and old. A long white beard hung from his strong jaw, and thick white eyebrows framed his beady, ice-blue eyes.

"Where are your manners, friends?" Devlin forced a laugh as he sat down near the hooded guest.

Clearly uncomfortable around the hooded man, the men also sat down – slowly, cautiously – all but one. A woodsman named Brison remained standing, with his sword still drawn.

Looking at the hooded man, but talking to Devlin, Brison said, "Stranger, you should not have invited *this* man."

As he spoke, he raised his right forearm, revealing a long scar – like a caterpillar.

"He is a dangerous magician, always conniving for his own best interest. He is angry and selfish. We cannot trust him."

The men at the fire began to talk among themselves.

Devlin countered in a loud voice.

"You say we cannot trust *him*? That's a strange complaint, coming from you Brison. You are chief among thieves in these woods, and *you* speak of not trusting?"

"These men know they can trust me," Brison replied, "You have misjudged me Devlin – I am no common thief. And, I have misjudged you. There is more to this game you are playing than you have shared.

With that, Brison stepped away from the fire and walked toward his horse.

"Where do you think you're going?" Devlin called after him.

"I am not interested in that man's help," Brison replied, without looking back.

"Brison," Devlin called again, "If we are going to succeed, we need another way. This man can help us. He comes in peace."

Brison stopped.

"No," he answered without turning around, "there is no peace in that man."

As Brison left, a few other men followed. The rest whispered to one another about whether to stay or go – most stayed. Soon, Brison and a few others had collected their things, mounted their horses, and were riding away – into the deep, dark forest.

All the while, the man with blue eyes remained silent, staring into the fire.

Frustrated and angry, Devlin shouted after them, "Cowards!"

His voice echoed in the forest. The fire crackled.

After a few moments, not even the clip-clop of their horses could be heard at the campfire.

Devlin turned his eyes to the hooded figure.

"I am sorry, Razo."

"It matters little. We do not need them."

The hooded man stood before the other men, looking them in the eyes as he asked, "Are you ready?"

"We are," they replied.

"Good," said the magician. "Prepare the camp. I believe Prince Winthrop is expecting us."

***

"Grandpa, who are these guys?" I interrupted the story. "They sound creepy."

"Yeah," Sissie joined in, "totally creepy."

Grandpa paused to look at us over his glasses.

"Indeed," he replied.

I could tell grandpa didn't like where this story was going. He knew Devlin, and seemed to know this Razo character. I could also tell, from the way grandpa's nose twitched, that Devlin and Razo both made him nervous.

This story already seemed more complicated than Drift's.

4

Map & Key

Back in his dreary cell, Winthrop careful unfolded a small torn piece of paper. It had appeared out of thin air, right in front of Winthrop, drifting from the top of the cave toward his hand.

Oddly, the paper did not surprise the young prince. Stranger things had happened in his father's kingdom.

In fact, Winthrop had been expecting something like this.

Four words stretched across the paper:

"The dragon is asleep."

"Finally," he grumbled, scratching at the thick leather bracelet on his wrist.

With a smug smile, Winthrop slid the paper into his pocket and walked toward the pile of rocks in his prison cell. Setting a few large stones aside, he dug out a small folded cloth and unfolded it. Inside, was a golden key and a tattered map.

Trusting that the dragon was asleep, Winthrop used the key to unlock his cell and then hid it in his pocket. Unfolding the map, the young prince headed out of his cell and into the cavernous, dark tunnels. If he hurried, he might see the sunrise.

***

"Wait, how could he have expected the note?" I asked.

"Yeah!" little Finn added. "Didn't we send it to him?"

"Grandpa, I'm a little scared," Sissie interrupted.

"I understand," grandpa replied. "Should we take a break?"

"No. It's okay," she whispered, "I want to know what happens next."

So, did I.

Grandpa looked back into the softly glowing pages.

***

Winthrop escaped his prison cell as quietly as possible – but every sound seemed to echo through the cave.

The mountain's ancient halls were tall and wide – large enough for the dragon to explore. Flickering light from the oil lamps threw dancing shadows on the ceiling.

Winthrop had to move quickly and quietly. At any moment, the dragon could wake. If that happened, all would be lost.

At each oil lamp, where it was a bit easier to see, Winthrop unfolded the map from his coat pocket and studied the path. This process repeated countless times as the young prince navigated the halls under the mountain. He walked in darkness, found a lamp, checked the map, and walked in darkness again until he found the next lamp.

After what seemed like hours, the tunnels began to narrow and the ceilings lowered. The deeper into the mountain Winthrop travelled, the fewer oil lamps he found.

His prison cell had been cold and damp, but here – deep in the mountain – the air was stale, warm, and dry. Winthrop was getting close to the heart of the mountain.

Then, it happened.

Walking in the dark, between oil lamps, Winthrop caught his toe on a raised stone in the path… and tripped.

Tumbling forward, the young prince tried to catch himself. Throwing his hands forward, Winthrop tumbled along the path with a crash. As he fell, the golden key slipped from his pocket and bounced along the stone path in front of him.

"Clink, clink, clink."

Winthrop listened as sound echoed, echoed, and echoed some more – moving from hall to hall, beneath the mountain.

Terrified, the young Prince froze.

"Clink, clink, clink."

The sound continued to echo – disturbing the silence under the mountain.

Suddenly, in a rush of wind and foul breath, another echoing sound filled the tunnels – a deep roar!

"Pesky child, you've interrupted my dreaming."

The dragon was awake.

***

"Oh no!" Finn squealed.

Leaning over our bunks, we kept our eyes fixed on grandpa – hanging on every word.

"He'll be okay, won't he grandpa?" Sissie whispered.

Grandpa didn't answer. I'm not sure he knew the answer.

He kept his eyes on the page. Was grandpa reading ahead silently?

"Grandpa," I asked, "Would you please keep reading? Out loud?"

Grandpa looked up with a wink and continued reading.

***

Quickly, Winthrop grabbed the key and jumped to his feet, shoving the key back in his pocket. He ran as fast as his legs could carry him – no more trying to walk softly.

In the distance, Winthrop could hear echoes of the dragon searching, seething, breathing, through each corridor of this lonely mountain.

At every turn, the tunnels narrowed. The young prince ran deeper and deeper into the mountain.

"Child," he heard the beast roar, "I hear you."

Winthrop kept running. In the distance, he spotted a faint glow of light. He ran toward it.

He could still hear the dragon racing behind him – banging into walls, knocking out lamps, chasing, hunting. Winthrop ran hard.

Around a bend, the young prince suddenly stopped.

He was standing in a large hall lit by several oil lamps. Across the giant hall, Winthrop could see three small doorways – big enough for a man, but far too small for a dragon.

Which doorway was he supposed to take?

The young prince ran toward the center of the hall. There was an oil lamp there. He pulled the map from his pocket.

He could hear the dragon closing in.

"Where am I?"

His mind raced through all the turns he had taken.

"Child," the dragon roared again, "I smell you."

***

"Grandpa, do we need to help Winthrop?" I blurted out.

42

The pages of the book flickered brighter.

"I'm getting scared," Sissie added.

Grandpa raised his eyes from the book and paused. Sissie wasn't the only nervous listener. All three of us were staring at grandpa, wide-eyed. In a few seconds, the dragon would catch up, and we had no idea how to help the prince!

"Children," he said softly, "I'm sorry. This story has not gone the way I remember it."

5

Dragon Chase

"What?" Little Finn blurted out, "You don't remember this?"

"No, and to tell you the truth, I'm a little nervous, too."

"Really?" I asked.

I thought he might be trying to pull our leg or something.

"Really, Riles," Grandpa sighed. "I don't know if we should have helped Prince Winthrop escape, but we did, and now he seems to be in even more trouble."

"But we don't know how to help him anyway!" Sissie said, "We don't know which path he should take."

"Good point, Sissie," I muttered. "Maybe we should listen to more of the story before we try to help."

"I like that idea, Riles," Little Finn added. "What do you think grandpa?"

"I think that's an excellent plan."

Grandpa smiled nervously, and continued reading.

***

Winthrop looked at the map, then up at the tunnels, then back at the map. Even with the lamp, he had trouble focusing on the map – with the dragon closing in – he just needed to choose.

His heart pounded out of his chest. His legs wobbled from racing through the cave. Trying to catch his breath, he tried to choose. He scratched at the bracelet on his arm.

The dragon was closing in.

He had to move. He still didn't know which path. He just needed to run!

Winthrop chose. As he turned to run, he caught his toe on a raised stone, and tripped again. For the second time today, the golden key flew out of his pocket. Reaching to catch it, he dropped the map too.

"Clink, clink, clink."

The keys echoed.

"Clink, clink, clink."

The dragon heard the key.

Turning a corner behind Winthrop, the scaly beast slid into the room with a crash and spotted the boy.

"Child," the dragon roared, "I see you."

Scrambling to his feet, Winthrop ran as fast as his legs would carry him. There was no time to pick up the key, or the map. The prince just ran.

The dragon closed in on Winthrop in just a few leaps and bounds. The stone room shook as Vigor's tail slammed against the ceiling and the wall.

Winthrop was just a step ahead as he lunged past the closest doorway. With a loud crash, the dragon's gigantic body smashed into the doorway, throwing stone and dust everywhere.

The dragon was too large to fit inside the door.

***

"He made it?" Finn asked, bursting with excitement.

"He made it!" I answered.

"Keep reading grandpa!" Sissie shouted.

So, he did.

***

Just inside the doorway, just beyond the reach of Vilgor, Winthrop kept running. Blind in the dark, he tripped a third time.

The young prince tumbled headlong down the dark, narrow corridor.

When he finally stopped rolling, he blinked his eyes but could see nothing. The corridor was pitch black. It was so dark that he couldn't see his own hands, or the stone beneath his feet, or the entrance he had tumbled through. Looking back up the path, he couldn't even see the angry, bruised dragon waiting impatiently at the doorway.

Meanwhile, Vilgor assessed the situation from the great hall. He could barely fit two nostrils into the opening, and his short, thick arms could only reach in a small distance. Collecting the boy would be difficult.

"Pesky pest of a boy," he muttered to himself, "I'll be glad when this is over."

Angry and annoyed by this whole affair, Vilgor imagined himself breathing a bit of fire down the tiny hallway, but that would do more than scare the boy. As much as he hated watching over this pesky prisoner, he needed to retrieve Winthrop alive.

Vilgor decided to wait. Eventually, the young prince would have to come out. He knew the prince was not brave, and the tunnel was both narrow and dark.

"It won't be long." Vilgor imagined. "The boy will return, afraid and alone. Then, I will put him back in his cell."

The mighty dragon curled up in center of the corridor, facing the doorway that held Winthrop. Exhausted from the chase, Vilgor fell back to sleep quickly. With each snore, he got closer to the beautiful dream Winthrop's pesky escape had interrupted.

Down the tunnel, Winthrop whimpered alone in the silent darkness – with no key, no map, no light, and only the distant company of an angry, snoring dragon. He scratched at the bracelet on his wrist.

***

"Wow, he really did make it!" Finn shouted again.

"He sure did, but now what?" I added. "No light, no map, no friends, and a dragon waiting to imprison him if he escapes!"

"Hey grandpa?" Sissie asked, "what's with the bracelet he keeps scratching?"

"Yeah," Finn added, "Why doesn't he just take it off."

"I'm not sure," grandpa replied.

"Well," I jumped in, "He definitely needs our help now, right?

The pages of the book glowed bright.

"Indeed," grandpa said quietly, "Winthrop will be frightened, alone in that tunnel. What would you like to do?"

"Hmm," Sissie thought out loud, "If we send Winthrop a note, he won't be able to read it. We need to find another way to help him."

That's when it hit me.

Hanging my head out of the bunk, I said, "I'm ready, grandpa."

I knew exactly what we could do to help the prince.

Sissie and Finn both looked confused.

"Ready for what?" Grandpa asked with a smile.

"You know, to jump into the story."

6

Riles Jumps

Grandpa chuckled, "Are you sure you want to try that again?"

"Riles, no! Absolutely not!" Sissie gasped. "There's a dragon in there!"

"Okay, *mom*," I replied – teasing Sissie.

She sure could be bossy at times.

"Listen, I'll be okay," I replied. "Just a few nights ago, Drift and I defeated space pirates with lasers. How's a dragon going to top that?"

"Um, he could breathe fire on you!" Finn jumped in.

"Oh, come on." I tried to laugh. "It's safe, isn't it grandpa?"

"Well, it's not as safe as you think," grandpa smiled. "You'll need to be careful. Vilgor *is* a dragon, and whether it's in a book or not, a dragon *is* a dragon."

Hmm. Grandpa's comment made be nervous. Was I ready? Maybe not.

On the other hand, heroes do all kinds of dangerous things, don't they? I mean, come on! This is what story keeping is all about.

More importantly, grandpa hadn't said "No" yet – and jumping into this dragon's tale would be so awesome!

I took a deep breath and exhaled slowly.

"Listen everyone," I looked around the bedroom, "if I'm going to do this we need a plan."

"Grandpa, please tell me you're not honestly thinking of letting him jump into this story,"

Sissie pleaded. "Seriously. There's a dragon in there."

"The dragon might be the least of his problems," grandpa replied.

"What?" I muttered back.

The dragon would be the least of my problems? What could that possibly mean? What did grandpa know? What secret was he keeping?

Grandpa went on, "However, I do like the idea of making a plan."

Sissie looked furious, but she knew better than to keep pushing the mommy act with grandpa. He never bought it. He liked adventure too much. She tried her hardest to keep me out of the book, but in the end, we all decided that jumping into the book really *was* the best way to help Winthrop.

Once she realized I was actually going to do it, she helped a ton – I guess she really didn't want that dragon to sizzle me.

We all put our heads together, and worked on a plan that would get me into the book, avoid the dragon, help Winthrop, and get home as quickly as possible.

While we were planning, grandpa told us a secret he learned while story keeping as a kid: you can take things into the book with you – as long as you make sure to bring it all back.

Little Finn ran out to the living room to collect a few things that might help me in the book – a flashlight, sunscreen, some M&Ms, a notebook, a pen, and little bit of toilet paper (just in case). He placed all the items inside a small backpack while Sissie, grandpa, and I sorted out a few final details.

When Finn returned with the pack, I was ready. We formed a tight circle around grandpa, and the book. The pages glowed soft white.

"Are you ready?" grandpa smiled at me.

Sissie grabbed my hand, gave it a small squeeze, and let go. I could tell she was nervous for me. I was mostly excited – but a little nervous too. The adventure with Drift had been amazing.

"I think so," I replied.

It was time.

"You've got this Riles," Finn smiled up at me.

"Thanks bud."

I reached one hand toward the book.

"Alright," I whispered, almost to myself, "here we go."

As my hand got closer, the pages grew even brighter. I can do this, I thought. I know what to expect this time.

I smiled toward Sissie, Finn, and grandpa, and then I laid my hand flat on the pages of the glowing book.

I didn't even have to press down. As soon as my hand touched the glowing pages, I felt a firm tug – just like I had a few nights before, with Drift's book.

The only difference? This time I got to enjoy it.

I took a deep breath and relaxed as the book's white glow wrapped around my body and sucked me into the book.

As I disappeared into the book I could hear Finn yelling: "Way to go Riles!"

"Grandpa," Sissie urged, "start reading. Quick!"

***

Winthrop felt a rush of cool air and closed his eyes quickly to hide them from a blinding white light that came out of nowhere. Riles landed hard on the cold stone floor in a swirl of light that left as quickly as it had arrived.

Terrified, the young prince backed tight against the dark stone wall. He could hear something else in the room breathing.

"Hello?" Winthrop whispered into the darkness, "Wh-who's there?" His voice stammered with fear, and his hand tugged at the leather bracelet on his wrist.

"A friend," Riles whispered back.

Riles rummaged through his pack and pulled out a flashlight.

"Devlin? Is that you?" the young prince whispered back.

"No." Riles whispered.

With a "click," the flashlight was on. Riles pointed it toward the ceiling of the tunnel and the two boys saw each other for the first time.

"Hey," Riles whispered.

7

Dragon's Eye

The young prince had never seen such a strong beam of light. It took a moment for his eyes to adjust.

"What do you want?" Winthrop whimpered, still tugging at the bracelet.

"It's okay," Riles assured him, "I'm here to help."

"How did you find me? Do you know Devlin? Did he send you?"

The young prince had so many questions. Riles didn't know where to start.

"Slow down Winthrop."

"That's *Prince* Winthrop to you," the boy replied in a huff, "and, how do you know who I am, anyway?"

Riles put his finger over his lips to shush the prince. Winthrop's jaw dropped. Did this manner-less boy just shush a prince? No one shushes a prince. Winthrop started to flush – bright red – though Riles didn't notice in the dark corridor.

"Did you just shush me?"

"Hear me out," Riles whispered, "I know that you're stuck down here – in the dark. I know there's a dragon guarding the doorway. I know you dropped your map up in the hall."

"I didn't drop it – it fell," Winthrop interrupted.

"Fine, it fell. Whatever. Truth is," Riles finished, "I'm here to help. Do you want my help?"

Winthrop nodded, "Yes."

"Alright, good." Riles whispered back, "I think dragon is still asleep. Do you remember where you dropped the map?"

"I didn't drop it, it fell," Winthrop bickered back in a whisper.

"Right," Riles rolled his eyes, "Do you know where the map fell?"

"I'm, I'm not sure." Winthrop stammered, "probably not far from the doorway, near the key – it fell too."

"Okay," Riles continued, "Why don't you hold this, and stay here."

Riles handed the flashlight to the young prince and wished himself to the top of the corridor.

In a flash of bright light, Riles disappeared into thin air.

Winthrop nearly dropped the flashlight in surprise and then muttered under his breath:

"So, he does know Devlin."

***

"Wait a sec," Finn interrupted, "Why does Winthrop think Riles knows Devlin?"

"I don't know, but that can't be good," Sissie chimed in.

Grandpa had a frown on his face.

"Do you think Winthrop saw Devlin flash – I mean like Riles flashes?" Finn added.

"Maybe," grandpa answered.

"Does that mean Devlin is like Lark?" Sissie asked.

"Let's hope not," replied grandpa, and then he kept reading.

***

In a second flash of light, Riles appeared near the opening of the corridor. The flash seemed extra bright compared to the dim room.

Looking into the great hall, he could see the dragon sleeping. In fact, it was the only thing he could see. Vilgor's huge body filled the whole corridor.

All the air inside the giant hall felt hot, thick, and smoky. Every breath Riles took burned his lungs.

Several oil lamps cast dim light around the hall, and every few seconds – when the dragon exhaled – sparks leapt out of Vilgor's gigantic nostrils as he snored.

Dragons snore? Riles could hardly believe it.

As terrifying as the whole situation seemed – standing in front of a sleeping dragon in the middle of this crazy story – the thought of a dragon snoring made Riles want to chuckle.

"Finn would think this was hilarious," he thought to himself.

Riles scanned the room, looking for the map. He didn't see it near the doorway, or near the dragon's head. He didn't see it near the other doorways.

It must be further away.

Riles looked down the hall, toward the dragon's tail. There, on the ground, he spotted it – something small and golden on the floor. From where Riles stood, it was difficult to see clearly. Maybe that bit of gold was Winthrop's key.

Riles *wished* himself to the far side of the beast.

In another flash of light, Riles disappeared from the doorway and reappeared next to the dragon's tail – just a few small steps away from the golden key.

Riles froze. Each time he wished himself somewhere new, the room lit up like fireworks.

Keeping one eye on the key and the other on the dragon, Riles wondered, "Could jumping around the room wake the dragon?"

Vilgor's head tilted slightly.

His leg twitched.

One wing stretched out just a bit.

Then, the dragon seemed to settle back in to a dream.

Relaxing a little, Riles quietly took one step toward the golden key. He scanned the stone floor for any sign of the map. Winthrop said it would be near the key.

The room felt silent.

Even the dragon seemed to hold his breath.

***

"Wait, what did you just read?" Sissie interrupted.

Grandpa paused, and then reread the last line, "Even the dragon seemed to hold his breath."

"Oh no!" Sissie squealed, "What if the dragon *is* holding his breath – he's going to get Riles!"

"The dragon's awake?" Finn shouted, "The dragon *is* awake!"

The book flashed bright, and grandpa continued reading.

***

Riles took a second step toward the key, careful to not make a sound. This time the dragon stirred just a little, sliding his tail several inches toward the boy. Riles didn't even notice.

The golden key was only one step away now.

The map was close too – just beyond the key.

Riles took a third step, leaned over, and grabbed the key.

Again, the dragon stirred just a little.

Vilgor's head tilted slightly – toward the boy.

Out of the corner of his eye, Riles noticed something drifting from the ceiling – a small piece of paper. What were Sissie and Finn trying to tell him?

Riles reached up and quietly caught the paper. Unfolding it, he squinted to read it in the dim-light:

"The dragon is awake."

Riles nearly stopped breathing. He froze in place.

Could it be true?

His heart began to beat faster and louder.

It became the loudest sound in the room: "dum-dum, dum-dum, dum-dum."

Just a bit further and he would have the map. Riles could almost reach it.

Vilgor couldn't really be awake, could he?

Riles watched the dragon.

One gigantic eyelid slowly opened, revealing one huge golden eye.

In a whisper, the dragon spoke:

"Child, I see you."

8

Devlin's Secret

Terrified, Riles lunged for the map. He snagged the ratted paper, fell to the stone floor, and rolled back to his feet.

Vilgor's tail tightened, his wing opened, and his arm stretched across a doorway, boxing Riles in on all sides.

Clutching the map, Riles *wished* himself back to Winthrop − and in a flash of white light, he disappeared.

In a blinding flash, the boy was gone.

"So, the white light has returned," Vilgor muttered – smiling as much as a dragon can, "This is good news. Good news indeed."

There would be no more sleeping for Vilgor – not now.

The dragon rolled quickly from his belly to his feet, lumbering upright. Then, he dashed toward the cave's proper entrance - his long tail swinging violently behind him as he raced through the halls.

The white light had returned.

He needed to tell *her* right away.

***

"Hold on grandpa," Sissie interrupted. "What did Vilgor mean about the white light coming back?"

Grandpa set the book down for a moment – his face nearly bursting into a wide smile. Grandpa could hardly contain himself.

"Grandpa?" little Finn asked, "Are you keeping something secret?"

"Well, maybe," grandpa replied. "Do you remember that I told you I've already read this book? That I read it with my father many years ago?"

"Yes," both children replied eagerly.

"Well, I've met Vilgor before."

Little Finn's mouth dropped, "No way, grandpa. You've met a dragon? That's crazy."

"Is that why you said we should give him a chance?" Sissie asked.

"I suppose so," grandpa replied. "Vilgor and I became very good friends a long time ago. Up until now I didn't know if he was still on our side."

"Our side?" the children asked together.

Grandpa nodded with a smile.

"What do you mean our side?" Sissie pushed.

"Well, some characters in this story are wonderful, but some are very dangerous," grandpa went on. "Until now, we couldn't be sure that Vilgor still supported the white light - the light I used to flash."

"Whoa!" Finn jumped in, "You and Riles flash the same color? That's awesome!"

Ignoring little Finn, Sissie asked, "What about the lady Vilgor is heading to see?"

"Good question," grandpa said, "but let's not get ahead of ourselves. We need to see what Riles is up to, don't we?"

Sissie and Finn exchanged glances. The more they read, the more questions they had - about the story *and* about grandpa.

"Alright," Sissie said, "Back to Riles."

Grandpa looked back to the book and continued reading.

***

In another bright flash, Riles reappeared next to the young prince. His heart was still pounding through his chest. That was a close call - a little too close.

Winthrop nearly dropped the flashlight. Surprised by the flash, he fell down against the wall and covered his face. Realizing it was just Riles, the prince jumped back to his feet.

"Well?" he whispered.

Riles held up the map.

"Excellent!" Winthrop smiled. Then he added, "What happened up there? It sounded like Vilgor said something, and then he stormed off."

"I'm not really sure," Riles replied. "I just grabbed the map and got out of there."

Riles took the flashlight from Winthrop and unfolded the map on the stone floor so they could take a look at it. Kneeling down in the dusty corridor, Winthrop started pointed out everything he recognized in the map - retracing his steps through the cave.

He seemed to know his way around the mountain - at least a little - so Riles let him take the lead.

"That awful beast unlawfully locked me in a prison cell over here," Winthrop whined, pointing on the map.

From there, the prince traced a path to the dark corridor they stood in, recalling the turns he took along the way and complaining about the dragon as often as possible. Finally, Winthrop looked up and said:

"We must be here. Now, how do we get out?"

The two boys studied the map in silence for a few minutes. Leaning in, Riles pointed to two places along the edge of the mountain - one near a forest and the other beside a lake.

"It looks like we could get out here, or here. Which exit do you think we should we head toward?"

The prince sat up and muttered - more to himself than to Riles, "If only I knew which place he wanted to meet."

Scratching at his leather bracelet, Winthrop turned toward Riles and asked, "Are you sure you don't know Devlin?"

Riles hesitated. He knew *about* Devlin - but it hadn't been a good first impression.

Grandpa had tried to warn them about helping Winthrop, and now it looked like the Prince and Devlin were working together. Riles wondered whether Winthrop knew the creepy magician too?

"Why do you ask?" Riles replied cautiously.

"Well, I thought Devlin was going to rescue me. I've been waiting for him, actually. So, I was a little surprised to meet you instead."

Riles nodded, not wanting to give anything away.

Winthrop went on, "Then, I saw you move around in a flash of light. Devlin does that too, it's just a different color."

Luckily, the flashlight was pointed down, or Winthrop would have seen a nervous look creeping across Riles' face.

***

"Wait, Devlin moves like Riles?" Finn interrupted.

Sissie's eyes got big. "Is he like Lark?"

Grandpa looked up from the pages, "I'm afraid so, kids. He's been inside this story before."

"Do you know him, grandpa?" Finn asked, surprised.

"Not really, but your parents do."

"How do mom and dad know him?" Sissie asked.

"I think I'll let them tell you that story, Sissie," grandpa winked.

"Oh man," Finn looked at grandpa nervously, "I bet Riles is scared. If I found out Devlin could jump around, I'd be totally freaked out!"

"Me too," Sissie added. "Is there anything we can do to help him?"

"Well, let's see what happens," grandpa said calmly. "I think Riles is doing a pretty good job so far."

Sissie and Finn nodded, and grandpa continued reading.

9

Fresh Air

"Umm," Riles tried to reply without sounding nervous. "Yeah, you figured it out. I know Devlin. It's kind of a secret. He doesn't know I'm here."

"Oh, that's great," Winthrop replied, still tugging at the leather bracelet. "He'll be so surprised!"

"You have no idea!" Riles sighed. "By the way, what's the deal with that bracelet? You're always scratching at it."

Winthrop looked down at his wrist - he *was* tugging at the leather bracelet, but he didn't know why.

"It was a gift," Winthrop smiled, raising his wrists into the light, "from Devlin."

"It looks like it hurts."

"No, it's just a bit itchy," Winthrop answered.

Riles, still staring at the bracelet, noticed strange writing leading up to one edge - it looked like "J-O-U."

"Any idea what those letters stand for?" Riles asked.

Winthrop glanced at the bracelet, shook his head, "No," and lowered the bracelet out of the flashlight's beam, "So, which path do you think we should take?"

"Right," Riles apologized, "Sorry for asking so many questions."

"It's alright," Winthrop looked down at his wrist.

Riles didn't know what to say, so he turned back to the map:

"About these paths..." Riles paused, "Last I remember, Devlin was meeting with some people..."

Riles closed his eyes for a moment and tried to picture what grandpa had read from the story. A campfire. A group of men. That creepy magician. Did that all happen in the forest? Riles didn't remember anything about a lake.

"Well?" the young prince asked impatiently.

He searched the map for a place that looked like what grandpa had read.

"I think they were meeting somewhere around here," Riles said, pointing to a small clearing near the edge of the forest. "Which path will take us that direction quickest?"

"This one?" Winthrop asked, pointing to a path not too far away that lead toward the forest exit.

"Great," said Riles, "Let's get started."

The two boys headed down the dark corridor - Winthrop scratching at his bracelet, and Riles following behind him, flashlight and map in hand. Riles couldn't take his eyes off that bracelet. Something about it seemed strange.

They walked for what seemed like hours, ran into dozens of cobwebs, and stubbed their toes on rocks left and right. Overall, the hike was pretty miserable and took longer than either boy wanted. Both Riles and Winthrop were starting to slow down - stomachs growling and exhausted from walking - when a cool breeze caught their attention.

It smelled like fresh air!

The boys lifted their heads, re-energized. They started to run. The tunnel brightened up as the outside light grew brighter. Glimpses of sunset colors reflected on the cave walls. Soon they would be free of this cave - out of the mountain!

Both boys slowed to a walk – catching their breathes. The prison cell, oil lamps, and gigantic dragon seemed like distant memories now. Here, the air felt cool and clean – not dusty and stale. Riles turned off the flashlight and returned it to the backpack.

"So, what's the plan?" Riles asked, slinging the pack back over his shoulder, "I mean after we meet up with Devlin?"

"You don't know?" Winthrop replied.

Riles smiled nervously, "Remind me."

"Well, he should have the army gathered by now, so once I join them, I suppose we'll be ready to march."

"March?"

"Yeah, march," Winthrop repeated himself, "to take the Kingdom."

"Right."

Riles tried hard to piece together the few clues he had. Devlin and the Magician wanted to free Winthrop - but why? Winthrop said they wanted to take over a Kingdom - but whose? And the bracelet - something about the bracelet bothered Riles.

Riles knew he didn't have the whole story - at least not yet.

"Ready?" Winthrop asked.

Riles nodded, "You bet."

Then, the two boys started running again – down the corridor toward fresh air.

***

Grandpa stopped reading and looked up with a smile.

"What's up grandpa?" Sissie asked.

"You kids are doing so well - I'm just really proud of you!"

"What do you mean, grandpa?" little Finn asked.

"I am having so much fun! A few minutes ago, you figured out that Vilgor's not so scary, and now Riles is inside the story - playing it safe and helping Winthrop at the same time!"

"Aw, thanks grandpa," Finn and Sissie smiled back.

Grandpa stood up from his rocker with the book in one hand and his empty mug in the other.

"Would you kids like to join me in the kitchen while I refill my tea?"

"Sure," Sissie and Finn replied.

Hopping out of their bunks, they followed grandpa down the hall. Sissie and Finn watched as grandpa heated more water and steeped his tea. All the while, Sissie couldn't stop thinking about Riles. Finally, she spoke up.

"Grandpa, I'm still worried about Riles. What's going to happen when he and Winthrop catch up to Devlin?"

"And that hooded guy?" Finn chimed in. "He seemed super creepy."

"Yeah," Sissie said, almost to herself. "What was his name?"

"Razo," grandpa answered. "His name is Razo."

"Do you know him too?" both children exclaimed.

"Yes, I remember Razo."

Sissie's mouth dropped, "Why didn't you say something earlier?"

She wasn't used to grandpa keeping so many secrets.

"I didn't want to ruin the story," grandpa chuckled, stirring sugar into his cream, "Razo was in this story way back when I was a kid. He is the most famous - and dangerous - wizard in all the land."

"What?" Sissie nearly screamed. "We have to warn Riles!"

Behind them, on the table, the book flipped itself open and pulsed bright with light. Only little Finn saw it.

"Umm, guys?" he tried to interrupt, eyes locked on the book, but grandpa and Sissie kept talking.

"Now, now," grandpa went on, "Don't worry so much Sissie. Riles learned so much with Drift. He knows how to jump around the story. I'm sure he can take care of himself."

"I'm not so sure, grandpa" Sissie replied. "Razo sounds pretty dangerous. A lot more dangerous than that pesky robot, AD-42."

On the table, the book pulsed bright a second time.

"Guys," Finn interrupted - a little louder - pointing at the book, "Are you seeing this?"

This time grandpa and Sissie did look. The book pulsed with light.

"The book seems worried. Should we send a clue?" Finn asked.

"I think Sissie already did," grandpa said with a smile. "Shall we see what happens next?"

Grandpa closed the book and slid it under his arm. Mug in hand, he headed back to the bedroom. Sissie and Finn followed, anxious to hear how things were going for Riles.

Sissie and Finn hustled into their bunks while Grandpa settled back into his rocker. Placing the book in his lap, grandpa let it fall open. Then, he continued reading.

10

Another Bracelet

Riles and Winthrop raced through the last few bends of the corridor and arrived at the cave opening before the sun had fully set. They took deep breaths, and smiled wide. The fresh summer breeze cooled their sweaty foreheads. It was good to be out of that mountain.

Standing at the entrance, the boys paused to enjoy the view.

Riles laid his backpack down, and stretched his arms in the cool evening air.

Perched above the forest, they could see a large valley open up below them. Looking east, the forest stretched almost as far as the boys could see. The sky was painted in beautiful streaks of red, pink, and orange.

Looking west, in the direction of the setting sun, Riles spotted a large castle tucked between the rising foothills and a lake on the valley floor. The castle seemed to overlook sprawling villages - as dots of firelight lit a path as far as he could see.

Winthrop noticed Riles staring toward the castle.

"That's my home." Winthrop said, scratching at his bracelet, "At least it used to be."

"It's beautiful," Riles replied, "Did the dragon steal you away from it?"

"Huh?" Winthrop turned toward Riles. "You really don't know what's going on here, do you?"

Riles forced a nervous smile, "What do you mean?"

Just then, Riles noticed a small piece of torn paper caught up in the evening breeze.

"A clue from grandpa?" he thought to himself.

As the paper circled near the entrance, Riles caught it, unfolded it, and read it to himself:

"Razo is dangerous."

"What's that, another clue?" Winthrop asked.

"Clue?" Riles whispered.

How did Winthrop know about paper clues?

"It's nothing," Riles added quickly.

"Nothing indeed," said a dark voice from around the edge of the rock.

"Finally!" Winthrop snapped, "Where have you been?"

"Your majesty, rescues take time and planning," said a second voice.

Two men stepped out of the shadows beyond the edge of the cave - both looked like silhouettes in front of the disappearing sun. Winthrop stepped toward the second voice.

"Where is my army?" Winthrop demanded. "And who is this hooded traveler accompanying you?"

***

"Grandpa, it's them!" Sissie blurted out anxiously.

Finn screamed at the book, "Jump!"

The book flashed bright.

Grandpa continued to read.

***

"Your majesty," said the dark voice, removing his hood, "I am at your service."

The old man wore a long white beard, bushy-white eyebrows, and steely-blue eyes.

"Razo?" Winthrop and Riles whispered in the same breath.

"Yes, Razo," said the dark voice, turning his wicked smile toward Riles.

Riles took a step back. The old man looked even more terrifying in person. The second silhouette stepped toward Winthrop.

"And, who is our friend?" he asked.

"*Our* friend?" Winthrop turned toward Riles, but stepped back, "He said he was your friend, Devlin."

Riles took another step away from everyone - this was not going well. Out of the corner of his eye, he noticed another paper circling in the soft breeze at the cave entrance - another clue!

Riles reached up for the paper.

When he did, something unexpected happened.

Devlin disappeared.

In a flash of dark red light, Devlin left Winthrop's side and reappeared next to Riles, locking arms with him before Riles could snatch the clue out of the sky.

***

"Whoa, Devlin just flashed red, like Lark!" Sissie asked.

"Yes," grandpa whispered.

"He can do that?"

Sissie could feel herself starting to panic.

Grandpa continued reading.

***

Riles - scared and angry - stared into Devlin's face. Devlin smiled back with a wicked, mocking smile.

As Devlin held Riles in place, the old magician sauntered slowly toward them. Bending low, he picked up the torn paper lying at Riles' feet - the clue meant for him. Dusting it off, Razo read it aloud:

"Jump!"

Devlin laughed, "Guess that won't be happening."

Riles could feel his heart pounding inside his chest.

He had to get home, back to grandpa.

Riles tried to jump out of the story.

A swirl of white light shot up around Riles and Devlin, lifting them into the air. At the same time, a swirl of dark red shot up. The two boys spun around briefly, before landing right where they started.

"Nice try," Devlin laughed, "I'm stronger than Lark."

Confused and afraid, Riles tried again, but the same thing happened.

He was stuck.

Riles tried to wrestle himself free. Devlin held tight, still mocking him with that wicked smile.

"Settle down young one," the magician whispered, stepping forward again, "there's no need to struggle. You've already lost."

Pulling a thick strip of leather from his cloak, holding it in front of Riles.

"Do you know what this is?" the magician asked.

Riles looked at the leather scrap.

It looked a lot like the one Winthrop wore.

"No," Riles whispered desperately.

Then, louder, "No!"

"Stop him Winthrop!" Riles screamed, struggling to break free of Devlin's grip,

Winthrop just stood there, watching and tugging at the bracelet on his wrist.

"Please," Riles begged, "the leather...it matches your bracelet."

Razo laughed, "Indeed it does, young friend."

Stepping close, the old magician placed the leather strap on Riles' arm, and like a fast-growing vine, the leather strip came to life, weaving itself around Riles' wrist.

Once the leather stopped moving, Devlin let go and Riles curled into a ball on the dusty ground, tugging at the leather on his wrist. His eyes welled with tears.

As he sat in the dirt, Riles stared at the bracelet. It had writing on it – four larger letters on the left edge, "R-N-A-L." Below them, on the other edge, were two smaller scuffed letters, "E.M."

Riles felt cold and afraid.

***

Grandpa stopped reading - his eyes still glued to the page, and his brain spinning.

"Grandpa?" Finn whispered, "What are we going to do?"

Grandpa didn't seem to hear Finn. He raised his reading glasses to a resting place on top of his head and looked toward the bunk.

"Children," grandpa whispered, "I'm beginning to understand these bracelets."

His brow furrowed as he thought.

"Grandpa, what about Riles?" Sissie asked. "He's in serious danger."

"Yes, of course," grandpa replied, "back to the book."

***

Realizing Devlin had let go of him, Riles tried to jump out of the story. Again, nothing - no swirl of white light, and no way home. Instead, he felt very, very afraid.

"Having trouble little one?" the wizard whispered through his wicked smile.

Riles glanced at Razo while he tugged at the leather bracelet. It wouldn't budge.

Razo reached toward Riles, curled up in a ball on the cave floor.

"Hand me the other clue, boy."

Riles reached a shaking hand toward Razo and dropped the torn paper into his outstretched palm. The magician unfolded it in his long, gnarled, fingers, and laughed as he read it aloud: "Razo is dangerous."

"This is true, little one, I am dangerous. But you knew that long before today, didn't you?"

A chill ran through Riles as the magician spoke. He didn't dare raise his eyes.

"You're not going home this time," Razo said in a cruel, dark whisper. "After all these years, I've finally caught you, Edward."

11

Grandpa's Secret

Grandpa nearly fell out of his rocker. His face was pale, like he had seen a ghost.

"How could this have happened?" he muttered to himself.

"Wait a second grandpa, what did Razo call Riles?" she asked, "He didn't know Riles' real name."

He called Riles something else, Finn interrupted, "Ernie? Edwin?"

"Edward," grandpa muttered.

"Right, Edward, that's what I said," Finn repeated.

"Why did Razo call Riles, Edward?" Sissie asked again.

"Because," grandpa replied softly, "Razo thinks he caught me."

"What?" Sissie gasped.

"I'm Edward."

"Come on grandpa," little Finn jumped in, "You're not Edward - you're Grandpa Eddie!"

"No Finn," grandpa replied, "Eddie is just my nickname. When I was your age I went by my given name - Edward."

"Oh no," Finn whispered.

"Umm, Grandpa - what else do you know about Razo?" Sissie asked.

"Like I said, he is a powerful and dangerous magician," grandpa said softly, "But I've never seen him try anything like this."

No one knew what to say. The whole situation was a terrible mess. Riles couldn't jump out of the book, and no one knew how to help him. Sissie, Finn, and grandpa sat together in silence for a few minutes.

Then, little Finn spoke up, "Grandpa?"

"Yes, Finn?"

"Will Riles ever get out of the story?"

"I hope so, but I'm not sure," grandpa weakly replied. "I've never seen this happen before."

"Well, it's up to us to help him!" Sissie blurted. "Grandpa, what are we going to do?"

"I don't know," grandpa whispered, "What do we know so far?"

"We need a plan," Finn suggested.

Sissie and Finn hopped down from their bunks. They agreed to take a few minutes to piece together everything they already knew about the story.

"Okay," Finn started, "when Devlin flashed, Winthrop and Razo weren't surprised at all, right?"

"Right," grandpa nodded.

"And Winthrop knew about the clues before we sent him one," Sissie added.

"Right," grandpa nodded.

"Didn't you say that you knew Devlin?" Sissie asked grandpa.

"Well, I knew *of* him," grandpa admitted, "According to your parents, he was trying to help someone take over the Kingdom. Your mom and dad jumped into the story to stop him."

"Grandpa! Are you telling us that Razo doesn't like you, and Devlin doesn't like our parents?" Sissie asked, sounding pretty annoyed, "Why are we reading this story?"

"Because," little Finn chimed in, "the book needs us, Sissie. We are Story Keepers, remember?"

"That's true Finn," grandpa said, smiling.

"Now," grandpa went on, "Listen up. I knew Razo all those years ago, but he never defeated me. I could always jump out of the story."

"So why couldn't Riles jump?" Sissie interrupted.

"I'm not positive - but," grandpa hesitated, "I think it has something to do with the bracelets."

"Of course, I knew those bracelets were fishy!" Finn exclaimed.

"What do you mean grandpa?" Sissie asked.

"Well," grandpa went on, "Do the two of you remember what Riles noticed about the bracelets?"

"You mean the writing?" the kids leaned in.

"Yes!" grandpa leaned forward too - getting excited, "Can you remember the exact letters he saw?"

Sissie and Finn had to think hard.

"Winthrop's bracelet only had 3 letters," Sissie recited, "*J, O,* and..." Sissie couldn't remember the third letter.

"Was it a *U*?" Finn asked.

"Yeah, good memory Finn," Sissie exclaimed.

"Okay, how about the other one," grandpa asked, "the one on Riles' arm.

"I think it started with an *R*," Finn started, then..."

"*N-A-L*," Sissie finished, "Plus the two small letters - *E* and *M*."

Finn ran over to the desk to grab paper and a pen. He tore the paper into two pieces, wrote out the letters for each bracelet, and laid the papers on the floor:

Riles: *RNAL* plus the small *E.M.*

Winthrop: *JOU*

"Wait," Sissie jumped down from the bunk, "What if you put Winthrop's in front...

JOU + RNAL

"Look! It spells journal!" Sissie giggled with excitement.

They were actually on to something.

"But, what about the E.M.?" Finn asked.

"I think I can help with that," grandpa interrupted. "Remember earlier, when I told Riles that anything he takes into the book needs to come back with him when he jumps out?"

"Uh-huh," Sissie and Finn nodded.

"Well, when I was a kid, I liked to take several of my favorite things into stories - things like my journal. One time, in this story, Razo almost captured me. We each had a hand on my journal when I jumped out of the story.

When I got home, I noticed the front cover was missing. I always thought it had burned up in the flash of bright light.

"Time to rethink that hypothesis, grandpa!" Sissie said with more laugh than sass, "It looks like that mean, old magician never let go of it."

"Oh, I get it!" Finn interrupted, "You're grandpa Eddie - the *E* is for *Edward*."

"Correct," grandpa went on, "and the *M* is for my last name - your mother's maiden name - *McAlister*."

Sissie could hardly believe it: "So, you're telling us that part of your old journal is now wrapped around Riles' arm?"

"It looks that way," grandpa replied.

Sissie, Finn, and grandpa wanted to keep chatting, but they were also worried about Riles. Grandpa picked up the book again, while Sissie tugged her bed-spread to the floor. She sat next to Finn, and threw the blanket over both of their shoulders.

This was going to be another late night.

12

Sissie's Turn

Once Sissie and Finn were snuggled up on the floor - wrapped in Sissie's bedspread - grandpa turned his eyes back to the book's soft glowing pages.

He adjusted his glasses and mumbled to himself, "Alright, where were we?"

***

"You're not going home this time," Razo said in a cruel, dark whisper. "After all these years, I've finally caught you, Edward."

"What's this all about?" Winthrop interrupted.

The prince looked almost as confused as Riles.

Razo stood to his full height and turned to face the young prince.

Despite all his arrogance, Winthrop stepped back afraid. The prince had heard stories about Razo - about his anger, and his power. Winthrop trusted Devlin, but not the old magician.

"Your majesty," Razo continued in a calm and calculated voice, "This man is a traitor - a spy from another world. I met him long ago - many years before your birth."

***

"What?" Sissie interrupted.

"He's not a traitor!" Finn hollered at the book.

It pulsed bright, and grandpa continued reading.

***

"Strong words," Winthrop said, remembering he wanted to be King, and feeling brave for possibly the first time, "especially for a twisted magician like you."

As he spoke, the prince noticed a small piece of torn paper circling in the breeze just over his head. Reaching up he caught the paper and read it aloud:

"He's not a traitor."

"Is that what the paper says or what you believe?" Razo asked in a quiet, steady voice.

The whole situation was very confusing for Winthrop. Riles had saved him, and secured the map. Riles had helped him out of the cave. He trusted Riles. He trusted the clue. But who was Edward? Winthrop found his strong voice again:

"Without this boy's help, I would not have escaped that horrible beast."

Razo countered, "No doubt that rescue was part of the traitor's plan, your majesty."

"That's ridiculous," Riles interrupted.

"You cannot trifle with dangerous spies," Devlin added, ignoring Riles, "They can be cunning tricksters."

"You're calling me a dangerous spy?" Riles shook his head in disgust.

"Do you even know the boy's name?" Razo questioned Winthrop. "Perhaps this boy is only pretending to help you so that later he can betray you."

Winthrop looked to Riles, and then to Devlin - unsure who to trust.

Devlin stepped toward the young prince, "Your majesty, do you not trust me? I have invited Razo to help our cause. You still want to claim your throne, don't you?"

He did. There was nothing the young prince wanted more than to be King. He could feel it as the magician spoke. He could see himself wearing the crown and ruling over the people.

"Yes, the kingdom," Winthrop muttered, scratching at his bracelet, "my kingdom."

"That's right, Winthrop" Razo said in a slow and steady tone, "We will make it your kingdom."

Riles watched all of this, still curled up on the cave floor – still afraid.

"Young Prince, we must go," Devlin spoke in the same slow voice, "This mountain is not safe. The dragon may already be looking for us, or worse, he may be warning the King of your escape. We must hurry to camp, where your army waits."

"Yes," Winthrop muttered, still scratching at the leather bracelet, "To camp. To my army."

Devlin took out a small rope and tied Riles' hands together. Then, tugging at his elbow, Razo lifted Riles to his feet and shoved him forward.

As Razo and Devlin made the boy a prisoner, Winthrop picked up Riles' backpack.

The four unlikely companions disappeared on a narrow trail behind the mountain and into the forest. Unable to flash, and without the energy to run, Riles marched in line with Devlin, Razo, and the Prince.

***

"Grandpa," Sissie interrupted, "This is terrible. Riles needs our help - and fast."

Her furrowed brow suggested she had a plan:

"It's time for us to do something."

"What do you have in mind?" grandpa asked.

"It's time for *me* to jump into the story."

"Oh no, we can't allow that," grandpa responded quickly, "It's far too dangerous, especially now!"

"But we have to help Riles!" Finn jumped into the conversation, "Sissie can do it!"

Finn was being mostly honest. He *did* think Sissie could do it. He *also* liked the idea of Sissie jumping into the story because the sooner Sissie got to jump in, the sooner he would get a turn.

"Absolutely not," grandpa replied.

"Grandpa," Sissie pleaded, "Hear me out."

"Fine, I'm listening, but make it quick."

"Alright. We know Vilgor is a friend because he said he likes the white light, right?"

"Yes."

"We also know that Vilgor went to warn someone about the Prince's escape."

"True."

We know that Riles can't jump, or run away, or get any of our clues without Devlin and Razo knowing about it."

Sissie was on a roll, and grandpa was listening.

"So, if I jump into the story with Vilgor...

"You can tell Vilgor's friend about Razo and Devlin?" Grandpa finished Sissie's sentence for her.

"It's the best chance we've got!" she added.

Finn agreed.

"That's an interesting plan," grandpa said softly - he sounded like he was actually considering it. "Are you sure you're ready?"

"Absolutely!" Sissie replied.

And, you're sure you *want* to do this?

"Yep," Sissie smiled wide.

"Sissie can totally handle this," Finn added, giving Sissie a high-five.

"Alright you two, I give in" grandpa smiled. "You came up with a very good plan - and it just might work."

"Thanks grandpa," Sissie smiled wide.

"You know what to do, right?" grandpa asked.

"Just touch the book?"

"That's right - whenever you're ready."

Sissie and Finn stood in front of grandpa's rocker, staring into the book. Sissie reached her hand toward the book. It was shaking just a little. Maybe she was nervous, maybe she was excited. Either way, this was an important moment.

"Wish me luck," she said as her fingers met the glowing pages.

Sissie closed her eyes and pictured Vilgor.

A white light shot up around her body.

In an instant, she was sucked into the story.

"Good luck," Finn and grandpa whispered as she vanished from the room.

Little Finn climbed into grandpa's lap, and they continued reading the story together.

13

Dragon Wings

In a swirl of light, Sissie fell to the ground, resting on soft, damp grass, looking into a sky full of stars.

"Hello little one."

The voice was deep and rich, like a warm roar - more safe than scary.

Lifting her head, Sissie saw the giant scaly body of a dragon all around her.

"Vilgor?" she whispered.

"It is I," the green beast replied. "You are a brave maiden, choosing to appear beside a dragon unarmed."

"But you know me, don't you?" Sissie replied confidently. "You know my white flash. You remember my grandfather - he was your friend."

"The white light is familiar. Your grandfather, you say?" Vilgor whispered in a soft, warm voice, "Do you mean Edward?"

"Yes," Sissie chuckled, "We call him grandpa Eddie."

"Edward and I were good friends years ago. I miss him dearly."

***

Grandpa paused a bit. His eyes filled with tears. Finn looked up, surprised.

"Are you sad, grandpa?"

"No Finn, happier than you could imagine. I miss Vilgor too."

Grandpa lifted his reading glasses, wiped his eyes, and continued reading.

***

The cool air gave Sissie a shiver as she stood drinking in the starry sky.

"Why are you here, little one?"

"I came to warn you, Vilgor," she spoke quietly, "And to ask for help."

"Warn me of what, little one?"

"My brother, who you met in the cave, has been captured."

"Hmm," Vilgor exhaled slowly like a purring cat. "That boy prince continues to cause problems he cannot understand."

Sissie's cheeks flushed with embarrassment.

"It wasn't all Winthrop's fault. My brother helped him escape the cave."

The dragon listened, patiently and without expression, as if he knew already.

"We thought that Winthrop was in trouble, you know?

Still, Vilgor listened.

"Riles and Winthrop reached an entrance to the cave at the same time as Razo and Devlin."

"Hmm. They are troublesome characters, aren't they?"

"Yes. I am worried for my brother," Sissie could feel herself getting anxious as she retold the story. "Devlin flashed, and Razo had a leather strap, and now Riles can't jump, and..."

"I understand, little one," Vilgor interrupted gently, "Why are you asking *me* for help?"

Sissie took a deep breath, "I know you are on your way to see someone - to tell *her* that Winthrop has escaped, or that the white light has returned, or both."

"Young one," the dragon replied, "It sounds like you have been listening well from your world. I *am* on that journey - to find the Lady of the Western Woods. Would you like to join me?"

"May I?" Sissie replied, grinning from ear to ear.

Vilgor rolled upright and stood on his hind legs. Lowering his left wing, the dragon beckoned Sissie to climb carefully onto his back. She did, settling just in front of his wings, at the base of his long neck.

"Are you ready, little one?" the dragon asked.

Sissie nodded.

With a great leap and several strong flaps, Vilgor shot high into the night sky. Sissie tucked in tight against his warm green scales and wrapped her arms around his neck. Her hair lifted in the cool evening air.

The view was magnificent. Wind in her face, Sissie scanned the expanding landscape as Vilgor circled into the clouds. Silver moonlight reflected on water, marking the rivers and lakes on the landscape below. To the East, Sissie could see a great mountain - maybe Vilgor's? It looked like a jagged triangle silhouette against the star-filled sky.

North and a bit west, Sissie could see the flickering lights of a city - and maybe a castle.

Westward, the last colors of day hid beneath the horizon. In between, stretched a large forest. Seeing the forest reminded Sissie of Riles.

"The sooner we find the Lady of the Western Woods, the better," Sissie thought to herself.

She couldn't bear the thought of Riles struggling in the forest.

Neither Sissie nor Vilgor said a word the entire flight.

The journey took several hours. They covered a lot of ground, carving a path over the great forest, toward distant rocky peaks. Looking back, past the dragon's tail, Sissie could barely pick out the giant mountain among all the growing shadows.

Midnight passed, and still they flew. The rush of cool summer wind tickled her face and filled her ears.

Then, Vilgor began his descent. Rocky hillsides dotted with evergreens came into focus.

The thick smell of Christmas lifted from swaying evergreen branches - dancing to the tune of a river that twisted through the valley and twinkled reflecting moonlight.

Vilgor glided just above the tree tops, twisting and turning between hillsides and rock outcroppings. Sissie didn't dare to close her eyes - afraid she might miss seeing something wonderful.

Finally, the mighty dragon gave another strong flap, pulling upright, and perched on a large bare rock.

Vilgor lowered his wing, and Sissie knew it was time to dismount.

She slid down the side of Vigor's wing and rolled headlong onto the cold, hard rock. It wasn't graceful, but she was on solid ground again. The dragon nearly laughed at her tumble.

"Did you enjoy the journey, little one?"

"Very much," Sissie replied, standing up and dusting herself off. "Thank you."

"It was my pleasure," the dragon replied. "Now, follow me. We must call on the Lady of the Western Wood."

***

"That was awesome, grandpa," Finn smiled, "Did you ever get to do that?"

"I sure did."

"Will I?"

"I hope so," grandpa replied.

Grandpa smiled back at Little Finn, whose eyes were growing heavy. He wondered if little Finn would stay awake for the end of this tale.

Either way, grandpa wasn't about to stop reading with two of his grandkids inside.

"Keep reading grandpa," Finn yawned.

14

The Lady

Lowering his large head, Vilgor lumbered toward the evergreen forest. Sissie followed. The large dragon moved quickly through the tall trees, occasionally knocking pinecones loose with his swaying tail. Sissie trotted behind Vilgor, far enough to dodge pinecones but close enough to keep up.

The moon kept their path well-lit as the girl and the dragon journeyed through the Western Wood. They walked for hours. Vilgor led the way, frequently choosing downhill turns. Sissie kept following - her legs aching with every step.

She could hear the sound of a river in the distance. With every step the sound of running water grew louder, lulling Sissie to sleep as they hiked deeper into the forest and lower into the valley.

At last, the forest thinned, and Sissie stepped into a large meadow. The changing scenery woke her spirits and she ran up to walk alongside Vilgor in the open space. The river was loud and close now. Just ahead of them, it cut through the center of the meadow, slicing the field in two.

Beyond the river, on the far side of the meadow, a rock cliff rose high above the thick evergreen forest. The rocky face glimmered like silver in the moonlight. At the base of the cliff, Sissie spotted an opening glowing with firelight. Her heart began to beat a little quicker.

"Is that cave her home?" she whispered

"Yes, little one. This way," the dragon replied. "She is waiting for you."

"Waiting? For me?"

Sissie imagined what it would be like to meet the Lady of the Western Wood.

Vilgor kept walking. It didn't take long to reach the river, but it was far too wide for Sissie to cross.

Sissie stepped to the bank of the rushing river, and watched as Vilgor waded in. The dragon paused halfway across and looked back at her.

"Are you coming, little one?" the dragon chuckled.

Stretching his wings from bank to bank, Vilgor formed a bridge for Sissie to climb.

May I?" she asked.

"Of course, little one."

Sissie scrambled onto Vigor's wing, crawled up to his body, and then slid back down the other wing - tumbling into the soft turf of the meadow.

"Well done, little one," the dragon smiled. "Much smoother than last time."

Crossing what remained of the meadow took even less time. Sissie and Vilgor headed straight to the flickering firelight marking the cave entrance. Their journey had taken much of the night, and the colors of sunrise were already peeking over the trees behind them.

Grandpa and Little Finn had sent no messages, and for all she knew, Riles was still in grave danger. Today, Sissie had a chance to be heroic - to get Riles home, and save a happy ending in this strange story.

Up close, the size of the rocky cliff made Vilgor look tiny. The dragon stopped at the cave's entrance, tucked in his wings, and curled up. Sissie stopped next to him and waited.

The dragon looked at her and laughed – as much as dragon's can.

"Go ahead little one," Vilgor encouraged Sissie, "She is waiting for you."

Sissie nodded.

She looked at the cave entrance.

"Be brave," she thought, and she stepped inside.

The cave narrowed quickly and turned to the left. Sissie walked in slowly, nervously. The cave had a cozy, worn out cabin feel to it - homey, albeit a bit untidy. Inside, the sound of the rushing river faded. Sissie could hear the distant sound of a woman humming.

"Hello?" Sissie called, feeling like an intruder.

"This way Elizabeth, this way," the humming voice replied.

"Elizabeth?" Sissie gasped, "How could she know my name?"

Sissie kept walking into the cave - toward that warm voice that new her name. Coming around a final corner, she spotted an old woman in a dark green cloak, standing on the far side of the room.

"Ah, there you are sweetheart."

The woman crossed what looked like a living room to offer Sissie a hug.

"You look just like your mother."

Sissie hugged the woman back.

"My mother? Do you know her?"

"Yes, of course deary. Come. Sit," the woman had a kind smile.

Working her way back to a cluttered wooden table at the center of the room, the woman used her arm to sweep a few knick-knacks off a wooden bench, clearing a space for Sissie to sit.

"How very rude of me - please make yourself at home."

Sissie followed and sat. The woman sat down across from her.

The cave was marvelous. A large oil lamp hung from a broad wooden beam stretching across the top of the cave. The lamp filled her whole home with warm light. Against the far wall a wood fire blazed inside an oven. The smoke vented up through several holes carved into the rock ceiling.

Along another wall, a straw mattress flowed over the edges of a modest wooden bed. Beautifully woven tapestries covered the dirt floor, and hundreds of books stood stacked like pedestals around the room.

The old woman removed her dark green hood. Her wispy gray hair flowed down her back - past her elbows - in a thick, loose braid. The woman's eyes sparkled green like emeralds, and her smile warmed the room more than the cooking fire or the lamp.

Sissie let out a long, deep breath. She felt comfortable and at home with the Lady of the Western Wood.

Forgetting Riles and enjoying the moment, Sissie asked, "How do you know my mother?"

"Sweetheart, that is a wonderful story which I would love to tell - but we must save it for another day," the woman gently replied.

"Yes, of course, I am so sorry," Sissie lowered her eyes to the table. She felt silly for asking.

"You need not be embarrassed," the Lady of the Western Wood said softly, smiling at Sissie, "You have traveled a long way to share important news with me. Tell me Elizabeth, why have you come?"

Sissie smiled.

For the next few minutes, Sissie told the Lady of the Western Wood her whole story. She talked about grandpa and bedtime, Winthrop whining in the cave, Riles grabbing the map, Devlin and

Razo showing up, the leather bracelets, and the flight with Vilgor. She talked quickly, but made sure to include every detail she remembered.

"Well," the Lady of the Western Wood said, sitting back in her chair, "It sounds like you've *all* had quite an adventure. Winthrop has behaved poorly, but his heart is not yet dark - perhaps we can still save him. When the time is right, that ambitious prince *will* make an excellent king."

Then, she added, "It's time for us to be brave together."

Sissie could feel excitement tingling in her fingers.

The Lady of the Western Wood went on, "Elizabeth, are you ready to be a hero?"

Sissie's grin reached ear to ear. She nodded.

"I'll take that as a yes," said the Lady, smiling back, "Let's go."

Grandpa paused reading to stretch. Little Finn had fallen asleep on his arm and it was starting to get tingly. As grandpa stretched, Finn started to wake.

"Grandpa, where am I? What's going on?" Finn mumbled, rubbing his eyes open.

"Easy Finn," grandpa chuckled, "Looks like you fell asleep while we were reading."

"Asleep? Where are Riles and Sissie?"

"In the story," grandpa smiled wide at little Finn.

"In the story?" he blurted, now fully awake, "What are you waiting for grandpa? Keep reading!"

15

Betrayal

Before Sissie met Vilgor and the Lady of the Western Wood, Riles had been captured.

He tried to jump home - right out of the story - but Devlin's strength and the leather bracelet kept Riles close.

Riles, Razo, Devlin, and the Prince headed down a narrow path. As they hiked down the mountain, Winthrop wondering who to trust, and Riles was too afraid to speak.

For the first few hours they walked by moonlight. Then, as they entered the forest, they continued in total darkness. Devlin and Razo talked a little, but always in whispers.

Curious sounds filled the forest - snapping twigs, rustling leaves.

More than once, Razo and Devlin stopped to listen. More than once, they suspected someone was following them. But, whenever the four hikers stopped to listen, the sounds seemed to disappear.

"It's nothing," Devlin would mutter.

Razo wasn't so sure.

The night sky had turned to pale blue when the forest thinned revealing a small meadow. They were close to camp, and several guards greeted them with hearty cheers. Winthrop received a few bows and "Your Majesties" from the men.

Devlin sent one of the guards back to camp to announce their arrival:

"Gather our leaders at the center tent - our new king has arrived."

Winthrop puffed out his chest and smiled wide. Finally, he would become King!

Another guard walked straight to where Razo stood holding Riles by the arm.

"Is this the boy?" he whispered.

"Yes," Razo whispered back, "Lock him in a cage behind the barracks."

The guard took Riles by the arm to lead him away. Exhausted and afraid, Riles did not try to fight back.

"One more thing," Razo added, "Check the forest. Someone has been following us."

The guard nodded, and led Riles into camp. Winthrop pretended not to notice.

"So, you're the lad who never ages," the guard taunted Riles, "Razo was hoping you'd show up."

Afraid, Riles kept his eyes on the path.

"You're quieter than I expected," the guard went on, "After all the stories Razo's been spinning about you, I thought you'd put up more of a fight. I guess he's already defeated you."

The guard led Riles to the edge of camp, behind the barracks, to a row of iron cages. Each cage was as wide as Riles could reach, and as high as his nose.

"Get in," the guard said, holding the first cage door open.

He shoved Riles inside, locked the door, and walked away without a word.

Once Riles was gone, Devlin led Winthrop and Razo to a tent in the center of camp. There, some of the top soldiers stood around a table, discussing battle plans over a map of the Kingdom.

Winthrop slipped off Riles' backpack as they entered the tent, and set it by the entrance.

"Gentlemen, update our Prince - what is the plan?" Devlin opened.

"Yes, of course," one soldier stepped forward and pointed on the map, "The King is strongest here. Some want to split our numbers and attack from two sides - here and here."

"We are too small to split our numbers," another soldier chimed in.

"I agree," said a third.

"Fine," said the first, "then our approach must be a surprise."

"What?" Winthrop interrupted, "No."

"Your majesty..." Devlin began.

"I will not take my father's Kingdom in secret," Winthrop continued.

Devlin glanced at Razo, and continued, "Of course, your majesty."

Then, Razo added, "Perhaps, young prince, we should let your generals plan for war?"

Winthrop felt his cheeks getting warm. Was Razo telling *him* how to run *his* army?

Turning toward Razo, he raised his voice, "I do not take orders from you!"

The old magician's eyes narrowed, but Devlin stepped in to settle them both.

"Prince Winthrop," he whispered, "Razo is only trying to help, and the plan is sound. We are few in number and will need a strong plan to defeat the King."

Winthrop scratched at his bracelet.

"I will not go to war like a thief in the night."

"Very well, my King," Devlin replied.

Razo nodded toward Devlin, and added, "If our services are not needed, we will leave you with you generals?"

"Yes. Go," Winthrop replied.

Once they had left the tent, Winthrop turned to the soldiers.

"We must fight with honor," he said, "Will you find a way?"

"Yes, King," they replied.

"Good, then I take my leave."

Winthrop stepped from the tent to follow Razo and Devlin. He definitely didn't trust the magician. He spotted them sneaking off at the edge of camp.

The young prince grabbed a dusty cloak from inside the tent, threw it over his shoulders, and raised the hood. Then, he followed Razo and Devlin into the forest. Hiding behind a slender elm, Winthrop watched and listened. He heard most of their conversation over the leaves rustling in the morning breeze.

"I *am* concerned," Devlin said.

"Nothing changes," Razo replied, "He still wears the bracelet.

"We need him to overthrow the King," Devlin whispered.

"He will," Razo whispered back. "Ruling is *all* he wants. It *controls* him."

"We cannot fail!"

"I understand."

Do you?" Devlin raised his voice, "Master Calamitous does not forgive easily."

***

"Master Calamitous?" Finn interrupted. "Isn't that the guy AD-42 and Lark talked about in Drift's story?"

"Yes, Finn," grandpa sighed.

"Do you know him, too?"

"I do," grandpa replied.

Then, he continued reading.

***

"I have *no* master," Razo muttered back.

"Do you want him *here* again?" Devlin mocked the magician.

Razo raised his staff, "Do not threaten me, boy - *you* came to *me* for help."

"Relax old man, we need each other this time," Devlin laughed at Razo.

"I own him," Razo repeated, "just like I own the white light."

"Finding the white light was lucky." Devlin cautioned, "Don't get careless."

"Perhaps," Razo smiled a wicked smile, "But, it was a lucky moment that I have been planning for many years. Come, the boy prince is awaiting his kingdom."

Devlin smiled too, "Shall we let him rule for a day before you take his crown."

"No. Not even for an hour," the magician muttered back, "Now, let's check in on Edward."

With that, Razo and Devlin headed back to camp, toward the barracks.

***

"Grandpa, they're heading to Riles." Finn looked up from grandpa's lap, "We've got to do something."

The pages hummed with their soft glowing light.

"What do you have in mind?"

"How about another note?"

Grandpa nodded, and the book pulsed bright.

Turning back to the book, Finn said in a firm voice, *"Be careful Riles, Razo wants to be King!"*

***

Winthrop watched from a distance. His heart sank. Razo *was* a traitor, and Devlin was no friend.

They were using him.

Young Prince Winthrop slumped down at the foot of the tree. There was no time to feel sorry for himself, and he couldn't fix things on his own.

He needed help.

Winthrop scratched at the leather bracelet - and for the first time, it moved.

He needed to find Riles - or Edward, or whatever his name was - and fast. Jumping to his feet, Winthrop followed after Razo and Devlin.

16

Fighting Fear

Riles sat slumped in a corner of his cage, afraid and feeling sorry for himself. As he scratched at the leather bracelet on his arm, a small piece of torn paper floated into his lap.

A smile crept across his face. A message from home? He unfolded the note:

"Careful, Razo wants to be King"

"Razo?"

Every time he thought about that magician, a chill ran through him.

He had never before felt so much fear.

It was time to be brave – to think.

Why did Sissie, Finn, and grandpa send him this clue?

Riles sat up and tried to list out everything he knew so far:

"If Razo wanted to be King," Riles thought, "He must be using Winthrop to get at the throne. But how? The bracelets?"

He looked down at his own wrist, still tightly wrapped in leather. What else could he remember?

"Devlin flashed red. He also knows Lark." Riles thought.

"Maybe, like Lark, Devlin works for Master Calamitous? That would explain why Devlin is helping Razo take over the Kingdom - he must want to ruin the happy ending!"

Riles' smile began to grow as he connected the dots.

"Why had Winthrop been in jail? He probably tried to overthrow the King. That would explain the guards that dropped off food every day."

Riles was on a roll.

"That means the King must be friends with the Dragon, and if the King is good, then the dragon is too!"

"Oh no! Riles paused. "We helped the wrong side!"

"Razo must be controlling the prince with the bracelet. That's why Winthrop expected Devlin and Razo to help him escape!"

Riles looked into the sky. Somewhere out there Sissie, Finn, and grandpa were listening.

"What now?" he shouted at the sky.

***

"Don't worry Riles," Finn said to the book. "Sissie's on her way!"

The book pulsed bright, and grandpa continued reading.

***

Riles, still looking up saw another small piece of paper falling out of the sky toward him. He also heard footsteps. Beyond the bend, two men were walking at the edge of the forest - coming his way.

It was Devlin and Razo.

Riles looked from the paper to the men, and then back to the paper. He jumped to his feet and stretched one arm up through the bars over his head, reaching for the falling note.

When the men saw the boy stand up, one started to run.

The paper wasn't falling fast enough.

Riles looked again - in a flash of red, one man disappeared. It was Devlin.

He looked back at the paper - just out of reach.

In a second flash, Devlin appeared on top of the cage and snatched the note.

Feeling brave for a moment, Riles grabbed Devlin's arm.

"Give it to me."

"Not a chance *boy*," Devlin teased, still catching his breath in the excitement.

Pulling his arm free, Devlin unfolded the note:

"Sissie's on her way."

"How sweet," Devlin laughed, "coming to save you I suppose? It won't matter. My work here is nearly done."

"You won't win, you know," Riles snapped, feeling braver still.

"Whatever," Devlin replied, grabbing on to the bars and looking down at Riles. He looked over his shoulder at Razo running to catch up.

In a whisper, he turned back to Riles and said, "I know you, Riles. I know you aren't your grandfather, and I know I can steal a happy ending from a runt like you any day of the week."

Riles didn't have a response.

He slumped down in the middle of the cage. Devlin was right - Riles had no strength, no plan, and no way to flash.

"Well, what did you find?" Razo asked when he finally caught up, "Why was Edward reaching through the cage?"

"Just a note, nothing to worry about," Devlin replied.

"I'll be the judge of that," Razo said, holding out his hand.

Devlin tossed the crumpled note to Razo and jumped off the cage. The old magician unfolded the note carefully and read it aloud:

"*Sissie's on her way.*"

"Hmm," the magician muttered, "I don't recall Edward having a sister."

Riles kept his eyes on the dirt. Just being close to Razo gave him the chills.

Devlin chuckled, "He doesn't."

Razo raised his eyes to Devlin, "What are you hiding?"

"That's not him," Devlin replied coolly.

"What do you mean *not him*?" Razo shot back, "Not the white light?"

"Not Edward."

Razo peered in at Riles with a cold stare.

"Who are you, *boy*?"

Goosebumps ran up and down Riles' arms. All his bravery hid.

He scratched at the bracelet, kept his eyes low, and said nothing.

"Answer me," Razo demanded.

Riles sat like a statue, frozen in fear.

Then, past Razo's feet, beyond his cloak, peeking around the corner of the barracks, Riles spotted Winthrop hiding.

Riles saw Winthrop wink.

A friend.

Some of the goosebumps disappeared. Maybe he wasn't alone.

"Who he is won't change anything," Devlin jumped in. "Come. We have work to do."

Razo kept his eyes on Riles.

Riles kept his eyes on Winthrop.

"Who are you?" Razo shouted, shaking the iron cage, "Answer me, boy!"

"Leave him," Devlin said again, "It's time for you to become King."

"Yes," the old magician muttered, letting go of the cage, "Let us make preparations."

Once the two men had wandered off, Winthrop hurried over to the cage.

"Are you alright?" Winthrop asked.

"I suppose."

"Look," Winthrop smiled, pushing his arm through the bars to show off the bracelet.

"It's loose!" Riles started to smile, "But how?"

"I'm not sure, but let me catch you up."

Winthrop sat down next to the cage and told Riles all about the argument with Razo in the tent, the plan to attack his father's Kingdom, and eavesdropping on Devlin and Razo in the forest.

"Of course, I want to be King," Winthrop said, "But while I listened to Razo and Devlin in the forest, I realized I'm not ready yet - no matter how bad I want it."

Riles smiled.

Winthrop went on, "I let those two trick me into this whole mess. A King can't let *that* happen, right?"

"Well Prince Winthrop," Riles put his hand on the Prince's shoulder through the iron bars. "Now you have a chance to write a different story. What's your plan?"

"Yes," Winthrop smiled again, "that's why I came to find you. I realized I can't do it on my..."

"Look," Riles interrupted in a whisper.

He pointed at the ground near Winthrop's feet. The young prince looked down. There, at his feet, was the bracelet. He didn't even feel it fall off.

Winthrop rolled his hand over. Where the bracelet had been, the young prince now had a long scar that looked like a caterpillar.

"How?" Riles asked, tugging at his own bracelet. It remained snug.

"I'm not sure," Winthrop replied, "but we will figure it out. I promise."

Winthrop grabbed the bracelet and tucked it into his back pocket.

"Thanks," Riles replied.

"What are friends for?" Winthrop smiled, "Now, let's get you out of here."

***

Little Finn looked up, "Grandpa, how did it happen? How did the bracelet fall off?"

"Maybe if we keep reading we'll find out."

"Okay," Finn fought a yawn. Part of him wanted to be in the book with Sissie and Riles - but the other part just wanted to sleep.

17

To The King

On the other side of the Kingdom, Sissie and the Lady of the Western Wood hurried back toward the cave entrance.

"Vilgor?" the Lady called ahead.

As they turned the corner, Vilgor's golden eyes slid open.

"At your service, friend."

"Thank you," the Lady replied. "Today we serve the King. Will you carry Elizabeth and I to *him*?"

"As you wish," the dragon replied.

The dragon stretched a wing toward them like a ramp. Both Sissie and the Lady climbed onto Vigor's back - Sissie in front, holding on tight.

In two great "swoops," they were flying. The meadow shrunk beneath them, and they shot toward the clouds. The Lady of the Western Wood hugged Sissie close and whispered stories about the kingdom, pointing out landmarks along the way.

"See those gigantic stones to the north?"

Sissie nodded.

"They mark Gallahan's resting place."

"Gallahan?" Sissie asked.

"Yes, a loyal giant who protected our land for many years. When the last war ended, he sat down at the foot of the forest, right there," she pointed, "and turned himself to stone. If you look carefully, you can count his toes."

Sissie nodded.

Looking south, she went on: "That is the Great River. She travels from my meadow to the heart of Vilgor's mountain, watering the open plains and Western Wood."

They flew over scattered villages and farms, patchy forests, rock outcroppings, and as the horizon shifted, Sissie spotted a tall peak rising above all other hills in the distance - Vilgor's home. A dark forest reached around the mountain's base like two strong arms.

Vilgor banked slightly left, and began to rise, carrying them over rocky peaks. Beyond the ridge, a new valley appeared along the Great River. The valley was dotted with villages.

Then, Lady nudged Sissie, and pointed east.

Across the Valley, tucked beyond a large lake, stood a tall castle. The same castle she spotted the night before. In daylight, it looked even more impressive. Vilgor banked again, heading straight toward the castle.

"Are you ready to meet the King?"

Sissie smiled.

She imagined herself walking through the stone halls or sitting at a large wooden banquet table. She imagined the King sitting on a large throne, dressed in royal robes, surrounded by knights. She imagined piles of jewels, and beautiful tapestries. Maybe, she would spot a princess or even a queen.

Then, she started to wonder if she would fit in. Sissie began to worry. Was she wearing the right clothes? Would she know how to act? Would the King agree to help Riles, or would he blame Sissie for helping Winthrop escape?

Her smile began to fade.

"Do not be afraid, Elizabeth," the Lady of the Western Wood leaned in and whispered. "He is a good King."

"How did you know what I was thinking?" Sissie asked.

The Lady of the Western Wood just smiled.

The castle grew larger as they flew closer, and Sissie could see archers on the castle wall. One soldier stood in a courtyard waving a large white flag with a green dragon on it. Vilgor headed toward the flag, and descended gently into the open courtyard.

Several knights greeted them.

"Welcome back Vilgor! Welcome Lady," one knight called up to them. "Who is your guest, and to what do we owe this unexpected visit?"

"We have urgent news for the King, Sir John" the Lady called back.

"Of course, Lady. We will announce your arrival."

Immediately, several knights hurried off to notify the King.

"Many thanks," she called back, in a very proper voice.

She scratched Vilgor's back just above his shoulder, and gave him a soft pat.

"Many thanks to you as well, friend," she whispered.

Vilgor stretched his wings for Sissie and the Lady to dismount. This time, Sissie landed on her feet. Vilgor turned his head to wink at her, and Sissie winked back.

Sissie followed the Lady and Sir John into a hall, at the end of the courtyard. After a series of twists and turns through the castle, they paused in front of a large wooden door. It was decorated with intricate carvings of knights and dragons, archers, magicians, and giants.

Sissie guessed that the carvings represented famous stories about the Kingdom. She wanted to hear those stories. She even wondered if grandpa was in some of them.

Suddenly, a trumpet sounded, and the large doors opened. They stepped into a tall room with beautifully woven carpet and three thrones. Several knights stood on either side of the carpet.

As the Lady of the Western Wood entered the room with Sir John, Sissie followed cautiously behind. At the far end of the room sat three chairs. The two on either side were empty, but rising from the center chair, was the King.

His light brown beard framed a strong, worn face. The King had light blue eyes and a soft smile. A golden crown rested atop his long, curly brown hair, but his clothes looked common -

dark green pants and a light brown top. Over his shoulders, he wore a hooded cloak of dark brown.

The King stood and walked toward them.

"Your majesty, I present the Lady of the Western Wood," said Sir John, as he stepped aside.

"Welcome," said the King, "What urgent news have you travelled to share?"

She bowed lightly, and stepping aside said, "It is *this* one who brings the news, your Majesty."

All eyes turned to Sissie. She looked at the King and bowed ever so slightly.

"Little one, what news do you bring?" the King repeated gently.

"Go ahead Elizabeth," the Lady of the Western Wood smiled, "this is your moment in the story."

Sissie drew in a long deep breath, then exhaled slowly. She had just enough courage to start the story. After the start, she found a bit more courage to continue, then a bit more to finish.

Sometimes being brave means having enough courage to start. Eventually, she had retold the entire adventure.

When she had finished, she saw tears in the King's eyes.

"Is Winthrop well?" he whispered.

***

"Grandpa," Finn interrupted, "We've got to tell him that Winthrop is safe - The bracelet fell off!"

The book pulsed bright.

Grandpa continued to read.

***

Before Sissie could answer, a small bit of torn paper fluttered to the woven carpet. Sissie picked it up and handed it to the King. Unfolding it in his fingers, he read the note in a whisper:

"The bracelet fell off."

"Is it true?" he asked.

"Yes, it must be." Sissie replied.

"Gather the knights," the King said to Sir John. "We will go at once. Razo has failed, and my son is free again."

Turning to Sissie and the Lady, he asked, "Will you wait here for our return?"

"No, your Majesty," she smiled. "We will go ahead of you. Vilgor wishes to protect the white light."

"Yes, of course," the King smiled back, "Together then, let us defend the white light."

Several knights stepped forward to fit the King with his armor and weapons, and the Lady ushered Sissie back through the halls to the courtyard where Vilgor waited.

Kneeling next to Sissie, the Lady said, "Elizabeth, Have you learned to move in white light?"

"No, not yet...I mean, I've never tried." Sissie whispered back.

"May I help?"

Sissie nodded.

"Take my hand, and hold onto Vilgor...excellent...now, imagine the place you read about - deep in the dark forest - where you first pictured Razo.

Sissie closed her eyes, and imagined that first campfire scene.

"Yes," the Lady smiled, "You're doing it."

In a swirl of white light, Vilgor, the Lady, and Sissie disappeared.

Under Siege

Just as Sissie and the Lady of the Western Wood arrived at the castle, Winthrop was breaking Riles out of his cage.

Winthrop grabbed a stone and banged on the lock.

After a few hard swings, the lock broke free. When Riles stepped out, both boys heard several loud horns blaring across camp - over and over.

Both boys made a dash into the forest and climbed to the lower branches of a tall elm. Along with the horns, they heard clanging metal and shouting men. Riles turned to Winthrop:

"What's going on?"

"I don't know. It sounds like an alarm."

There was another sound Riles didn't recognize - a high pitched, soft whistling. Winthrop recognized it at once - the sound of arrows. Razo's camp was under attack. The boys climbed a bit higher so they could see over the barracks.

A band of about a dozen men were pushing into camp from the north. Devlin's small army seemed surprised and confused - running into tents to grab shields and swords.

The boys watched the scene unfold from halfway up the elm tree.

Chaos swallowed the entire camp in minutes. Flaming arrows shot out of the forest, drawing red and orange arcs in the pale morning sky. The arrows landed in tents along the north edge of camp – setting them ablaze. The burning tents sent pillars of dark smoke into the sky.

That wasn't all. Devlin's army had scattered. Now, they were returning with shields and swords. At the north end of camp, men on both sides ran at each other, swinging swords and axes.

As the attackers pushed into camp, Winthrop pointed out a strong looking woodsman on horseback. He seemed to be signaling to the other attackers - leading them.

The attackers were winning. Inch by inch, they took over the camp - pushing in from the forest edge. Winthrop and Riles watched in amazement. Neither boy had seen a battle like this - up close.

Then, Winthrop spotted a single flaming arrow high above the rest. It landed on tent in the center of camp - where he had argued with Razo and Devlin. The tent burst into flame.

That's when Winthrop remembered… "The backpack!"

***

"Oh, no!" Finn looked up at grandpa, "They can't leave it, can they?"

Little Finn remembered grandpa's warning.

Grandpa sighed, "No, everything we take into a story should return home."

Finn shouted at the book, *"Don't leave it!"*

The pages pulsed bright, and grandpa continued reading.

***

"What did you say?" Riles asked.

"The backpack!" Winthrop repeated, "I left your backpack in that tent."

"That's fine," Riles replied, "We won't need any of that stuff now."

As Riles spoke, Winthrop noticed another bit of paper drifting toward them through the elm branches. He snagged it.

"Can I read this one?"

"Go ahead," Riles smiled.

Winthrop unfolded the note and read:

"Don't leave it."

Riles smiled nervously, "Well, I guess that means we need to get the backpack."

Winthrop, who felt much more like himself now that the bracelet had fallen off, hurried down the tree.

Riles followed more cautiously. He didn't know if he had the courage to face that old magician again. Riles scratched at his bracelet. The two boys peered into camp from the forest's edge.

"Follow me," Winthrop said, "I think I can get us to the tent without being seen.

Riles nodded and followed.

Winthrop ducked in and out of other tents, making his way toward the center of camp. They moved north across the camp, toward the battle, noise, smoke, and fire.

Peeking around one tent, they could see all the way to the north edge of the forest. The woodsman was still there, on horseback, directing his men to attack. Razo's army seemed totally confused. The center tent was just ahead – it's canvas door hung shut.

"Ready," Winthrop asked.

"I think so," Riles said, faking a smile. He felt afraid, but there was nowhere else he could go.

The boys darted across the last open space and slipped inside the tent.

Flames worked their way up the canvas walls across from them, and a light haze of smoke made it difficult to see clearly. The tent looked empty.

Winthrop pointed to the right, and they spotted the backpack right where he had left it. Riles grabbed the pack and slipped it over his shoulders. Without a word, they ducked out of the tent, and began sneaking back to the forest edge.

That's when Razo and Devlin spotted them.

"Look," Razo flashed his wicked smile, "you know what to do."

Devlin nodded, and disappeared in a flash of red light.

The boys ran hard until they reached the edge of the forest - then, they slowed to a walk.

"What an adventure," Winthrop smiled at Riles, "I've never been that close to battle before."

Riles faked another smile. He wanted to share Winthrop's enthusiasm.

"Where to now?" Riles asked, still scratching his bracelet.

Before Winthrop could answer, a flash of dark red light startled them - Devlin.

Riles and Winthrop turned and ran - along the edge of the forest, away from the battle and away from Devlin.

Another flash - Devlin stood ahead of them again, laughing.

"Where do you think you're going?"

"Not with you!" Winthrop shot back. "You traitor."

As Winthrop yelled, Riles looked around for Razo. The old magician stood ahead of them at the edge of the forest.

Another chill ran through Riles. Tugging at Winthrop's hand, Riles turned to run deeper into the forest.

Devlin flashed ahead of them, "Not so fast."

Riles turned again, heading toward camp. Winthrop followed. Looking up, he realized they were running straight toward Razo.

The boys turned again. This time Riles caught his foot on a root and tripped as Winthrop ran by. The backpack fell off. Razo closed in.

"Come on!" Winthrop yelled.

Riles froze.

Winthrop ran back and pulled him to his feet. Riles grabbed the pack, and they both ran.

They didn't notice the backpack was open.

They didn't see the pack of M&Ms fall out.

Razo did.

Neither boy looked back, as they ran toward the south end of camp - along the edge of the forest.

Another flash of dark red light — Devlin blocked their way.

"Enough."

The boys stopped - out of breath and sweaty. It was no use. They couldn't outrun Devlin or the old magician.

***

"It's okay," little Finn shouted at the book, *"Vilgor is coming!"*

Grandpa smiled. Little Finn was doing an excellent job of "story keeping."

***

Razo caught up the to the others just as a small torn paper fell through the forest canopy. The boys watched as Devlin took the paper, unfolded it, and read aloud:

"Vilgor is coming."

Under all of his fear, Riles felt a spark of hope, deep inside.

Not far away, in a flash of white light, Vilgor, Sissie, and the Lady of the Western Wood appeared at the base of the dragon's mountain in a quiet clearing.

"Can you smell them?" the Lady asked Vilgor.

"Yes, friend," the dragon replied, "and I smell battle."

"Then we must hurry," she replied.

She and Sissie climbed onto the dragon's back, and with a leap, they were off.

19

Facing Fear

Back at camp, Razo mocked Winthrop and Riles.

"That foolish dragon. He always was a friend of the white light."

Devlin stepped closer to the boys, flashing his wicked smile.

"He'll be too late this time," Razo cackled, raising his magician's staff, "This ends now."

"Not so fast," came another voice from the forest.

Razo froze. It was the woodsman.

Slipping off the horse, he stepped toward Riles and Winthrop, holding his sword.

"Leave us," Devlin yelled, "this does not concern you, Brison."

***

"Brison?" Finn interrupted.

"Of course!" grandpa smiled wide, "He has returned!"

"Wasn't he at the camp in the beginning?"

"Indeed," grandpa answered, "He refused to join Razo."

"Why did he come back?" Finn asked grandpa.

Grandpa smiled, "Let's find out," and continued to read.

***

"Doesn't concern me?" the woodsman replied to Devlin, "There is much you do not know, young traveler."

Turning to Razo, Brison raised his left arm, revealing a long caterpillar shaped scar, stretching from his elbow to his wrist. Just like Winthrop's scar.

For the first time, Razo looked afraid. Both he and Devlin took a step back.

"I warned you Devlin," Brison continued, stepping toward them, "There is no peace in that old magician."

As he spoke, more than a dozen other woodsmen stepped out from the trees. Riles shot Winthrop a smile - more hope.

"Do you really think you can take the boy from us?" Devlin sneered with a wicked smile.

As he spoke, a great shadow moved across the forest, blocking the sun - Vilgor had arrived.

Devlin looked up at the dragon, and around at all the woodsmen. Then, he grabbed Razo by the arm and they both disappeared in a flash of dark red light.

The woodsmen hurried around the boys in small circle, and Brison lowered his sword.

"Are you alright?" he asked.

"Yes, thank you," Winthrop replied, "How did you find us?"

"Young prince," Brison laughed, "we are woodsmen, and you are in our woods."

The other men laughed as well.

"Sir, I mean, Brison," Winthrop asked, "May I see your scar?"

Brison took a knee and held out his left forearm. Winthrop held out his own arm, revealing the same caterpillar scar.

"I suspected as much," said the woodsman, "And you, white light?"

Riles held out his arm - the bracelet still firmly wrapped on his wrist.

"Hmm. I am sorry, little one."

"Can you help him?" Winthrop asked.

"No," Brison replied, "It is not my place."

As they chatted, one of the woodsman leaned whispered in Brison's ear, "Sir, we have company."

Brison stood as two of the woodsmen escorted two women into their circle. All the woodsmen took a knee.

As soon as Sissie spotted Riles she ran across the circle and knocked him over with a massive hug. Winthrop helped them up and Riles quickly introduced the prince to his sister.

The Lady of the Western Wood walked over to Brison,

"Thank you, Keeper of the Forest."

"Of course, my Lady," he replied and bowed.

196

Kneeling again, Brison called Winthrop over and placed a hand on his shoulder:

"Young prince, do not forget this day or your scar."

All the other woodsmen disappeared into the forest. Winthrop nodded. Then, Brison disappeared with the others.

Winthrop turned to the Lady.

"Are you..."

"I am," she answered.

"Wow," was all he could say.

"Boys," she went on, "I want to show you something."

Then, rolling up her left sleeve, the Lady of the Western Wood revealed a narrow scar of her own. It was shaped like a caterpillar and climbed from her wrist toward her elbow.

All three children stared, silent.

"You are not alone, young Winthrop," she whispered.

"Neither are you," she added, turning to Riles, "now, follow me."

The three children followed her back toward camp. Winthrop could hardly believe he was with *her*. Until this moment, he had only heard stories of the Lady of the Western Wood from his father. Riles walked a step behind, with Sissie, still anxious to avoid Razo. He scratched at the bracelet while Sissie recounted her adventure.

As they reached the forest edge, an incredible sight opened up. Nearly all the tents burned bright. Vilgor swooped back and forth breathing destruction on Razo and Devlin's dream.

"Do something!" Devlin shouted.

"What would you like me to do?" Razo shouted back, "Your army is fleeing, and we are only two against this beast!"

"Enough," Devlin yelled back, "I am no coward."

In a flash of red, he disappeared.

He reappeared on Vilgor's back, swinging and kicking. Vilgor spun, breathing fire across his own tail. Devlin let go, falling to the ground. Then, he disappeared in a flash – reappearing high on Vilgor's long neck.

The dragon swung his head left and right, trying to shake the rider. Devlin held on tight with his legs and used his hands to swing punches at Vilgor.

Throwing his head back, the dragon shook Devlin loose a second time.

Halfway to the ground, Devlin disappeared in another flash, and reappeared at the end of Vigor's tail.

"Enough!" Vilgor roared.

With a strong tail-whip, he tossed Devlin straight toward the burning center tent.

"Nooo!" he shouted as he fell.

And just before he crashed into the tent, Devlin disappeared in a final dark red flash. This time, he did not reappear. Vilgor scanned the camp, but there was no sign of the red light anywhere.

Vilgor landed at the edge of camp and locked eyes on Razo. All the other men laid down their weapons in surrender.

"Stay back beast!" Razo yelled, pointing his staff.

"I am not afraid of an old magician," Vilgor snarled, "Where is the white light."

As the dragon spoke, the Lady of the Western Wood approached, with Winthrop, Riles, and Sissie.

"He is here, Vilgor," the Lady called out, "He is safe."

Razo turned and noticed the bracelet still clinging to Riles' wrist.

With a wicked smile, he added, "Not safe just yet, is he."

Riles winced, as an icy chill ran up his spine - so much fear.

Then, a trumpet interrupted them. Winthrop recognized it at once - the King had arrived. Galloping into place, the King and his knights completed a circle surrounding Razo and his men.

Winthrop ran across the circle to his father.

"Daddy," he burst into tears, "I am so sorry."

The King knelt, and held Winthrop in his arms, "I know son, I forgive you."

The Lady of the Western Wood turned to Riles.

"This is your moment," she whispered, "Are you ready for it."

Riles' feet felt heavier than stone. He looked around the circle - Sissie smiled, Vilgor lowered his head, and even the King gave a nod.

He felt the spark of hope begin to burn. He took a step forward - toward Razo. The fire inside burned a bit stronger, so he took another step.

Razo turned to the boy, "You may not be Edward, but you are mine."

"No," Riles thought.

Razo continued, "You will always fear me."

"No," Riles whispered, feeling braver each moment. He looked to Winthrop who smiled back.

"What's that boy," Razo shouted.

Riles felt the same icy chill in his spine, but this time it didn't freeze him. He turned to the magician, and saw him for what he was - a wicked and angry man. Then he realized the truth: Razo never controlled Riles, fear did.

"I said, No," Riles stood tall, "I am not afraid of you."

He felt the bracelet loosen on his wrist.

"I am not afraid of you," Riles repeated, "and I am not alone."

As he spoke, the bracelet slipped off his wrist, landing in the dust at his feet. Riles looked at his wrist, and saw a short, thick scar shaped like a caterpillar.

He was free.

20

Home Again

Grandpa paused his reading to check in with little Finn.

"What do you think about that?" grandpa whispered.

No reply.

"Finn?" grandpa whispered a little louder.

Nothing but heavy breathing. Poor little Finn had finally fallen asleep.

Grandpa smiled, and continued reading on his own. It was time to bring the children home.

***

As the bracelet fell off Riles' wrist, the crowd erupted in cheering. Sissie and Winthrop even ran over to give Riles hugs. Finally, he was free.

The King gave orders to his knights, "Arrest these men for treason - and be careful with the magician."

It took just a few moments for the knights to round up all the men, collect their weapons, and bind their hands. Getting back to the castle presented several other challenges. It would take a full day to march the prisoners to the castle, but it was already late afternoon. Setting up camp for the night would be risky - everyone wanted to see Razo behind bars as soon as possible.

Some suggested sending a few knights to ride ahead and return with more horses. Others thought the dragon should help carry people back and forth. In the end, it was Riles who offered the best idea.

Everyone - prisoners and knights, royalty and dragon, Riles, Sissie, and the Lady - held hands or feet or tails. Two knights paid special attention to Razo, making sure he couldn't run off. Then, Sissie closed her eyes and imagined herself in the castle courtyard.

In a swirl of white light, the whole group disappeared from the forest and reappeared in the castle courtyard.

Cheers broke out a second time, celebrating Riles and Sissie. The white light had returned, and again the Kingdom was restored.

Immediately, the prisoners were carried off to prison cells, leaving the rest to celebrate.

Knights led Razo, without his staff, to a solitary cell deep inside the castle. There, they untied his hands and locked him in the cell.

Once he was alone, Razo slid a strange package from his cloak pocket - the M&Ms. He tore one end open, and peeked in at the brightly colored candies, a wicked smile creeping over his face.

"This is not the end Edward," the old magician muttered, "I will find a way. Just you wait."

***

Grandpa pulled his eyes from the pages. Was Razo talking to him?

He looked down at Finn, still sleeping in his lap.

Then, taking a deep breath, he kept reading.

***

Back in the courtyard, the celebration continued.

The King sent courtiers this way and that, preparing food and drink, decorations and games. The whole Kingdom would be invited to celebrate the return of the Prince.

Vilgor, who had not enjoyed a proper sleep since Winthrop's escape, was eager to return to his cave. As the dragon gathered himself to leave, Winthrop, Riles, and Sissie interrupted.

"Wait, please!" they called out.

"Yes, children?" he replied, lowering his head to the ground level.

"You're not leaving, are you?" Sissie asked.

"I am, little one," Vilgor replied, "It is time for us to say goodbye."

Sissie reached out to touch the dragon's nose, and he swooped her up on his neck and lowered her back down."

"I'm going to miss you Vilgor," Sissie smiled.

"I will not forget you, child," the dragon replied, "Send my love to Edward too."

Sissie curtsied, and then stepped back. The boys remained.

"Yes, children?" the dragon asked.

"Well, it's just that…" Winthrop started.

"We'd like to apologize," Riles finished.

"Yes, Winthrop continued, "I know that I have behaved beastly…I mean, terribly to you."

"And," Riles added, "I never should have snuck into your cave, or assumed you were bad - just because you were a dragon."

"I understand," the dragon nodded, "You children have learned much in this adventure."

The boys nodded.

"Perhaps we will meet again," Vilgor added, "and be friends from the start."

Then, he leapt into the air and made his way home.

Across the courtyard, Sissie sat with the Lady of the Western Wood. Riles and Winthrop hurried to join her.

"Hello boys," she said when Riles and Winthrop arrived, "Have you made your peace with the dragon."

"Yes, Lady," they replied.

"Good," she smiled.

Then, the King interrupted, "Winthrop?"

"Yes, Father?"

"Come quickly, it is time to prepare for the festivities!"

"Yes, Father," Winthrop replied, "May I say my goodbyes?"

The King made his way to where they sat.

"So, our friends cannot stay for the party?" the King laughed, "I should have expected as much."

"I must decline, your majesty," the Lady smiled. "It is time for the white light to return home."

"Indeed," the King said, still smiling, "My Lady, it is always a pleasure. Children, I can only hope we meet again."

Riles and Sissie agreed - both very much hoping they would have another chance to explore this Kingdom. After more hugs and goodbyes, the King and Winthrop headed down a castle hall and the children were left alone with the Lady of the Western Wood.

"Well, children," she whispered, "there's one more thing I'd like to show you. May I?"

Riles and Sissie both brimmed with enthusiasm. Standing between them, the Lady of the Western Wood took their hands into her own.

"Ready?"

"Yes," they replied.

A swirl of green light wrapped around their bodies and in a flash, they disappeared.

Grandpa nearly fell out of his chair with a chuckle.

"Oh-ho-ho, she did it!" he laughed, "I knew she could still do it!"

Finn rolled over in grandpa's lap.

"What's going on grandpa?"

"Nothing, Little Finn," grandpa chuckled, "nothing at all."

Grandpa helped Finn settle back into sleep, and continued reading.

In another green flash, Sissie, Riles, and the Lady reappeared near the table at the center of her cozy cave in the Western Wood. Sissie burst out laughing.

"You can flash like us!"

"Yes, Elizabeth, I most certainly can," she replied.

"Riles, she knows my name - I mean my real name," Sissie laughed, "And she knows mother, too!"

"You do?" Riles asked.

"I do," the Lady replied, "But I'm afraid tonight is not the night for that story."

Riles and Sissie looked at each other confused.

"Will we see you another night?"

"I imagine so, she said with a twinkle in her emerald eyes, "And when you get home, give Edward a big hug for me."

Sissie and Riles leaned in, fighting back tears, and gave the Lady of the Western Wood a big hug. Then, stepping back, they whispered,

"Goodbye."

In a flash of white light, Riles and Sissie disappeared from the cozy cave.

***

In a flash of light, Sissie and I tumbled out of the book and onto the floor.

What an adventure!

I was so happy to be home - I kissed the bedroom carpet, and the bunk bed, and anything else I could reach.

Grandpa closed the book and stood holding Finn.

"Welcome home," he whispered, "It's been quite a night for us all."

Sissie and I nodded. We ran over to give him hugs.

Grandpa tucked Finn into the lower bunk, while Sissie and I took turns going to the bathroom. Pretty soon, we were tucked in too.

Leaning in to my bunk, grandpa whispered, "Let's take a peek."

"What do you mean?" I asked.

Gently, grandpa held my left hand and rolled it over - the caterpillar scar - it was real, even outside the book.

Grandpa smiled, "It certainly was a crazy adventure."

"It sure was," I smiled back.

"You'll both drift to sleep quicker than you can imagine. Adventures like tonight's are exhausting – trust me."

"We believe you, grandpa," Sissie and I whispered.

Grandpa tucked us all back into our bunks, gave us hugs and kisses goodnight, and headed to the door.

"Get some sleep. There's no telling what new adventure is waiting for us tomorrow."

21

Tomorrow

And with a wink, grandpa left the room. I got the feeling grandpa knew exactly what adventure was waiting for tomorrow.

Part of me wanted to stay up just to hear Sissie's adventure, but grandpa was right – I was tired, and there would be plenty of time to talk tomorrow. So, I closed my eyes and fell asleep in no time.

The next morning Sissie, Finn and I slept in way longer than normal. Eventually, our grumbling stomachs made enough noise to wake us and we all trudged down to the kitchen for breakfast.

Grandpa was already there, cooking up eggs and pancakes.

"Finally decided to get up, huh?" he laughed, as we slid onto the dining table bench.

Then we saw it.

Right there on the table.

Another book.

Ready for more Story Keeping?

I know what you're thinking: "It can't end there!"

Don't worry, it doesn't.

Find out what happens next...

- ✓ Will our Story Keeping heroes jump into another book?
- ✓ Will they meet Agent Lark again?
- ✓ What about Master Calamitous? Is he still trying to ruin happy endings?
- ✓ Does Grandpa know more than he is telling?
- ✓ And where did their parents really go that summer?

Two Requests:

1. Would you be willing to leave a review on Amazon? It'd be a HUGE help!

2. Don't forget to snag your FREE GIFT at *www.armarshall.com/storykeeping*

96332699R00130

Made in the USA
Columbia, SC
25 May 2018